EXCITEMENT, SUSPENSE—AND KAY TRACEY—GO TOGETHER!

Sixteen-year-old Kay Tracey is an amateur detective with a sense of sleuthing that a professional might envy. Her closest friends who share her adventures are Betty Worth and her twin sister Wendy. Whenever there is a mystery in the small town of Brantwood, you'll find Kay and her two friends in the middle of it.

If you like spine-tingling action and heart-stopping suspense, follow the trail of Kay and her friends in the other books in this series: *The Double Disguise, In the Sunken Garden, The Mansion of Secrets, The Green Cameo Mystery* and *The Message in the Sand Dunes.*

Bantam Books by Frances K. Judd
Ask your bookseller for the books you have missed

THE DOUBLE DISGUISE
IN THE SUNKEN GARDEN
THE SIX FINGERED GLOVE MYSTERY
THE MANSION OF SECRETS
THE GREEN CAMEO MYSTERY
THE MESSAGE IN THE SAND DUNES

A Kay Tracey Mystery

THE SIX-FINGERED GLOVE MYSTERY

Frances K. Judd

A BANTAM SKYLARK BOOK

THE SIX-FINGERED GLOVE MYSTERY
*A Bantam Skylark Book/published by arrangement with
Lamplight Publishing, Inc.*

PRINTING HISTORY
*Hardcover edition published in 1978 exclusively by Lamplight
Publishing, Inc.*
Bantam Skylark edition/October 1980

ISBN 0-553-15082-0

Published simultaneously in the United States and Canada

---

*Bantam Books are published by Bantam Books, Inc. Its trade-
mark, consisting of the words "Bantam Books" and the por-
trayal of a bantam, is Registered in U.S. Patent and Trademark
Office and in other countries. Marca Registrada. Bantam Books, Inc.,
666 Fifth Avenue, New York, New York 10103.*

PRINTED IN THE UNITED STATES OF AMERICA

0 9 8 7 6 5 4 3 2 1

BOOK DESIGNED BY MIERRE

Contents

THE SIX-FINGERED
GLOVE MYSTERY

Kay struggled to get out of her prison

I

The Black Glove

"It's starting to snow, Mother," Kay said, as she glanced out of the window into the night.

Mrs. Tracey, an attractive woman in her early forties, looked up from the suitcase she was packing. She and Kay were going to spend Thanksgiving with Aunt Jane.

"I hope the roads won't be icy," Mrs. Tracey said uneasily.

At that moment the door bell rang several times. Mother and daughter looked at each other, slightly startled, for whoever it was seemed quite impatient.

"I'll answer it," Kay said quickly.

Opening the door, she was amazed to see her good friend Betty Worth in a torn and muddy coat.

"What on earth happened to you?" Kay cried, grasping her friend by the arm.

"I—I was hit by a car!" Betty sobbed.

Mrs. Tracey and Kay helped Betty to a sofa in the living room, where they cleaned the cuts on her face.

"What happened?" Mrs. Tracey asked gently.

"I was on my way over here and I was crossing at the intersection at Rockwell and Fulton when I saw a big tan car speeding towards me. I tried to get out of the way, but as the driver slammed on his brakes his fender grazed me."

"You could have been killed!" Mrs. Tracey said, shuddering.

"The driver wouldn't have cared if I had been," Betty said bitterly. "He didn't even stop to see if I was all right."

"Why, that's a criminal offense!" Kay cried. "Did you get his license number?"

"No. By the time I realized what had happened the car was gone."

"You're sure the car was tan?" Kay asked.

"Yes, I noticed that much about it."

"Was anyone else in the car?"

"I only saw the driver. I got a glimpse of his face. He was mean looking."

"Can you describe him at all?" Kay asked.

Betty shook her head. "Everything happened too fast. If I hadn't jumped backwards I could have been killed. That driver should be arrested!"

"There's not much chance of that," Kay said regretfully. "Without his license number, finding him will be impossible."

"I'm just glad to be alive," Betty added. "Oh, where is my purse?" she cried, looking around her.

"You didn't have it when you came in," Kay told her.

"I probably dropped it somewhere in the road."

"We'll go look for it as soon as you've rested," Kay suggested.

Betty was still quite shaken up and, at the moment, not too concerned about her purse.

"It's not worth worrying about. There was nothing but a little change in it."

"Nothing else?" Mrs. Tracey asked.

"Oh yes, and three theater tickets. I almost forgot about them."

"Then the purse is worth looking for," Kay said firmly. "I'm going to look for it right now."

Despite Betty's protests, Kay rushed off to the scene of the accident to look for the purse.

"It doesn't matter," Betty insisted when Kay returned empty-handed. "Someone probably picked it up right after the accident."

"Did you have any identification in the purse?" Mrs. Tracey asked.

"I think so. But I'd be surprised if the purse were returned."

"You'll probably never see it again," Kay agreed. "But you may be able to find out who picked it up."

"How?" Betty asked eagerly.

"Do you remember the seat numbers on the theater tickets?"

"I know they were aisle seats in the first row of the balcony."

"Then all you have to do is to watch those three seats at the play on that night. If they're occupied, you'll know who took your bag."

"That's a great idea," Betty said enthusiastically.

"I just wish we could track down that driver. He shouldn't be allowed to get away with this!"

When Kay phoned the Worth residence to let the family know about the accident, it was Betty's twin sister, Wendy, who answered the phone. Mr. and Mrs. Worth were out for the evening, but Wendy was going to rush right over.

While Kay was on the phone, her cousin, Bill Tracey, had come home after working late in his law office. A bachelor, he had lived for many years with Kay and her widowed mother.

"What's happened?" Bill asked as he looked down

at Betty, who was still pale and somewhat shaken.

When Kay and Mrs. Tracey had filled Bill in, he asked if anyone had notified the police.

"Not yet," answered Kay.

Bill promptly called the police station, repeating all the information Betty had given him.

"I am afraid the police won't be able to be of much help," he said. "We just don't have enough information for them."

At that moment Wendy arrived at the front door. Breathless from running she rushed into the living room to see Betty.

"Are you all right?" she cried at the sight of her sister's pale, drawn face.

"I feel fine now, thanks to Mrs. Tracey and Kay. But I lost my purse, and our theater tickets were in it."

"I don't care about the tickets. Tell me exactly what happened."

The story was being repeated for the third time when the doorbell rang again.

When Kay opened the door, she found herself face to face with a policeman and a beautiful young woman in a sable coat. The policeman asked if they could come in.

"Are you the young lady who was hit by a car at Rockwell and Fulton?" the officer asked Betty.

"Yes," she replied weakly.

Turning to the woman at his side, he asked Betty, "Have you seen this lady before?"

"I don't think so, but her face is somewhat familiar—"

"I am Beatrice Ball," the young woman said, introducing herself.

"The famous actress," the policeman added.

Miss Ball smiled. "I'm not sure about the 'famous' part, but I am an actress."

"Did you see Miss Ball riding in the car that hit you?" the policeman asked.

"Oh, no," Betty answered. "I only saw the driver."

"Don't be afraid of implicating me," the actress said quickly. "I'm certain I was in the car—in the back seat with my hands tied."

"Your hands tied!" Kay gasped. "Had you been kidnaped?"

"Yes, shortly after I left the hotel on the outskirts of Carmont where I had been staying, I had my chauffeur stop to pick up something at a store. Suddenly this tan car drove alongside. At gunpoint I was ordered into the car."

"Did you see the driver's face?" Bill asked.

"No. He wore a mask. Later on, as we drove through a lighted street, he removed it, but his back was then toward me. He raced toward town. Suddenly I heard the brakes screech. Then we hit something."

"That something was me," Betty commented.

"The accident seemed to frighten the man. He became very distracted and I was able to work my hands free. As he slowed down for a corner, I tried to jump out."

"That was a brave thing to do, lady," the policeman said, "but mighty dangerous. You could have been killed." Then, turning toward the door, he added, "I'm going to have to report back to the Captain. See you later."

After the officer had left, Miss Ball resumed her story.

"I didn't stop to think of the risk I was taking. Just as I clutched the door handle, the kidnaper swung the car to the curb and grabbed my wrist. We struggled, and I managed to free myself."

The actress paused in her narrative as she suddenly

remembered something. She opened her purse and pulled out a black object.

"When I got away I realized I had this in my hand," she added excitedly. "Maybe it will help locate the driver."

She held out a man's black glove. As the group looked at it, Betty said wearily:

"I don't see how."

"It's not much good except maybe to show the size of the driver's hand," Wendy added.

The actress looked disappointed. She had hoped the glove might be a clue.

"Can I see the glove?" Kay suddenly asked.

"It's just an ordinary glove," Mrs. Tracey remarked as she glanced at it.

"It's anything but that," Kay said. "Take a close look at it, Bill."

"A glove with *six fingers!*" Bill exclaimed, his eyes wide with amazement. "I've never seen such a thing!"

II

A Diamond Ring

"You're very observant, Kay," said Bill. "We all looked at that glove, and not one of us noticed the extra finger."

"A man with six fingers would certainly be easy to identify," Mrs. Tracey commented, picking up the glove and then tossing it on the table again.

"If he can be located," Bill added.

"Now that we have some evidence, Kay'll find him all right!" said Wendy confidently.

Kay was carefully inspecting the glove. Miss Ball was quite upset when Kay tried it on, leaving the empty finger to dangle.

"Oh, take that awful thing off," Betty pleaded. "It gives me the creeps."

Kay pulled the glove off slowly. When she did withdraw her hand, she held a tiny object between her thumb and forefinger. With delight she held it up for the others to see.

"A ring!" Betty gasped. "And it's a diamond!"

"Clue number two!" Kay announced. "It was wedged in the tip of the third finger. When Mother tossed the glove on the table a moment ago I heard it clink against the wood."

"You ought to be on the police force, Miss Tracey," said Miss Ball admiringly. "This has been quite a night. It would make a wonderful play. And now I must go."

Miss Ball was about to leave but she looked so exhausted Mrs. Tracey urged her to stay. The actress sank wearily into a comfortable chair and closed her eyes.

"You've had a traumatic evening," Betty said sympathetically.

"Yes, we both did. My nerves are pretty shot. For a time the excitement kept me keyed up, but now I feel drained."

"You must stay here for the night," Mrs. Tracey urged.

"Oh, no thank you, I couldn't do that. I really must go soon. Can I use your telephone?"

"Certainly. Kay will show you where it is."

"I want to let my manager, Clarence Minton, know what's happened. He's in New York," Miss Ball explained.

"Any chance that the kidnaper could be someone who knows you or Mr. Minton?" Kay asked.

"It's possible," Miss Ball admitted.

"Mr. Minton might be able to help us identify him," said Kay.

"Well, I intend to tell him all about the ring and the glove. He may have some ideas."

Kay showed Miss Ball to the telephone and then returned to the living room. Miss Ball was charming, yet unaffected, and during the short time she had spent in the Tracey home had endeared herself to everyone.

"After this, I'm never going to miss a single one of Miss Ball's movies," said Wendy. "She's so beautiful she reminds me of a poem by Lord Byron:

A Diamond Ring

"'She walks in beauty, like the night
Of cloudless climes and starry skies:
And all that's best of dark and bright
Meet in her aspect and her eyes.'"

Although Betty and Wendy were twins, they weren't at all alike in either appearance or personality. Wendy had dark hair and tended to be serious, while her sister was blond and playful. Betty was not as studious as Wendy, and did not share her love for poetry.

Kay had the reputation of being the best amateur sleuth in the area. Once she had stumbled upon a mystery which she solved so expertly that all of Brantwood marvelled and thereafter people sought her out whenever they had mysteries nobody else could unravel. Ingenious and observant, Kay had not failed to solve a single one.

At sixteen Kay was tall and slim, with brownish-gold hair and deep brown eyes. Her face was pretty and very expressive.

Kay attended Carmont High School. Together with Wendy and Betty she traveled the few miles each day from Brantwood, their home town, to school. They had many friends among their classmates, but Chris Eaton was not one of them. Chris was always trying to make trouble, particularly for Kay whose popularity she resented. However, Kay had better things to do than worry about that. Important things like helping Miss Ball.

"Good news!" the actress announced as she returned to the living room after making her phone call. "Clarence is coming here immediately to try to help us find the kidnaper."

"Great!" Kay cried. "When will he get here?"

"He's leaving in ten minutes to take a plane. He should get in late tonight."

"I insist that you stay with us until he comes," Mrs. Tracey said.

Not wanting to impose, Miss Ball hesitated. However, when Kay and Bill joined in the invitation she finally agreed to stay. Since it would be several hours before Minton arrived, Miss Ball was persuaded to lie down and get some rest.

Betty now felt well enough to go home and Bill offered her and Wendy a ride.

Kay went along. Returning home in the falling snow, she had an idea.

"Let's go by way of Rockwell and Fulton. I'd like to take another look for Betty's purse."

"All right," Bill agreed, turning down a side street. "I have to make an important phone call so I'll run into that drug store down the block while you go up and look around."

Bill parked the car and Kay jumped out.

"I'll only be a minute," she said, as she hurried up the street.

She darted around the corner, then stopped short in her tracks. A tan sedan was parked not far from the intersection where Betty had been hit.

"I wonder if that's the same car that hit Betty?" Kay thought.

She glanced at the rear license plate, but it was too muddy to be legible.

The engine was running, but the car was empty. Kay looked up the street and was startled to see a man examining the scene of the accident.

Even from a distance there was something sinister about the man. He was tall and thin, and moved with a jerky stride. His black hat was pulled low over his eyes, so Kay could not see his face.

Kay noticed his hands, which were particularly large and clumsy. Also, he wore only one glove.

"He could very well be the man we're looking for!" Kay thought.

Then, as a brilliant idea occurred to her, she ran back to Bill's car.

III

A Radio Warning

Kay was breathless with excitement when she reached the car. Bill was just coming out of the store.

"I think I may have seen the man who hit Betty!" she told him as she slid into the car. "At least, he fits the description. Drive slowly around the corner."

Bill didn't waste any time asking questions. However, when they reached the intersection, there wasn't a soul in sight.

"Maybe you were mistaken," said Bill.

Kay shook her head. She'd definitely seen that tan car parked by the roadside, and as evidence she pointed out a few drops of dark oil which marked the place where the car had stood only a few moments before. But the car was gone now, and the mysterious stranger with it.

As she looked down the street, Kay could see a dim tail-light far in the distance.

"That must be it, Bill! Let's follow him!" she cried.

Bill took up the pursuit. As Kay peered anxiously through the snow-encrusted windshield, she was certain the tan car was just up ahead.

"Can't you go a little faster, Bill?"

"The roads are pretty slippery but I'll try to speed up a little."

But they just couldn't get any closer. It was obvious the driver was aware he was being followed, and was trying to elude his pursuers. When they reached Carmont, he led them quite a chase down several side streets. His behavior convinced Kay and Bill that they were on the trail of the right man and they were determined not to let him escape.

While the tan car sped past red lights and stop signs, Bill refused to drive so recklessly, and began to lose distance. But when he saw the car turn into a one-way street, he saw his chance.

"Speed up, Bill, and we'll catch him!" Kay cried.

They were now so close to the car that Kay could almost make out the numbers on the grimy license plate.

But as they approached the end of the street, a large truck suddenly backed out from the rear exit of a garage, directly in the path of Bill's car. Bill slammed on the brakes, swerving just in time to avoid a collision.

The startled truck driver climbed out from behind his wheel and hurried over to apologize.

"I'm sorry, sir. This street is seldom used at night, so I often back out without looking."

"That's a bad habit," Bill snapped. "Just get your truck out of here as quickly as you can! We're following another car!"

"Yes, sir." The man ran back to his truck and moved it so that Bill could pass.

When they came to the corner, Kay and Bill peered in both directions but the street was deserted.

"Now we've lost him," Kay said. "If it hadn't been for that truck we would have caught up with him."

"We'll never find him now," Bill admitted. "We may as well give up."

"Let's go to police headquarters and let them know we've seen the car in this neighborhood," Kay suggested. "Maybe the cruiser will be able to find it."

"That's a good idea. We're not far from the station now."

When they arrived at the precinct they told the officials about their pursuit of the car. The information was immediately relayed to the radio cruiser.

Convinced they'd done all they could, Kay and Bill returned home. Mrs. Tracey met them at the door asking that they be as quiet as possible so as not to wake Miss Ball.

"She's exhausted by her experience," Mrs. Tracey said.

"She should have a little of Kay's iron nerve," said Bill, giving Kay's cheek a playful pinch.

"It's way past your bedtime, Kay," Mrs. Tracey commented, as she glanced at the clock. "You have school tomorrow, you know."

"Oh, Mother, can't I go to the airport with Miss Ball!"

"But the plane will be coming in very late."

"I won't be able to sleep anyway, so you might as well let me go."

"Yes, I know you, Kay," her mother said, smiling.

"Kay's the detective on the case," Bill piped in, "and we'll need her around, should anything turn up."

Kay gave each of them a hug. Then she whirled her mother about the room so fast that Mrs. Tracey got dizzy and fell onto the sofa.

"I declare, Kay, you're as frisky as a two-year-old."

"It's just my way of working up steam for the big attack," Kay laughed, but her face sobered as she said it. "I'm not really satisfied with the way this mystery is progressing."

"What's the matter?" Bill asked. "You've made a good start already, getting two clues."

"But it's only a start," Kay replied. "I have a feeling that the man who lost the glove will be difficult to capture."

It would be a while yet before their drive to the airport so Mrs. Tracey and Bill settled down with some reading. Too excited to sit quietly for any length of time, Kay jumped up to look at the clock every few minutes.

"We ought to leave soon," Bill finally suggested. "If we don't, Kay will wear out the carpet, the way she prances about."

Miss Ball was awakened, and as soon as she was dressed they all left in Bill's car for the airport. By now it had stopped snowing, but it was bitterly cold.

"Mr. Minton is brave to fly in this weather," Mrs. Tracey remarked to Miss Ball, as they approached Carmont airport.

"Yes, he is," replied Miss Ball. "I hope he gets here safely. I've been so worried about this trip."

Kay glanced quickly at the young woman, wondering about the nature of her relationship with Minton. It seemed to go beyond business.

They parked near the runway and waited for Minton's plane as great sheets of wind-driven snow blew across the field.

"I understand engine failure is not uncommon in weather like this," Miss Ball murmured apprehensively.

"Mr. Minton will get in safely. Don't worry," said Bill.

Miss Ball appeared to grow more and more nervous as time went by. Finally Bill suggested that they go inside the terminal to see if there was any news on the incoming plane.

"Any news about flight 417?" Bill asked the operator.

"She was running on schedule at the latest report. It's almost time for another check-in. If you'll wait—"

Bill nodded.

There was a brief pause as the operator tuned in. Then came the indistinct call:

"4—1—7; 4—1—7."

Miss Ball listened tensely, twisting her handkerchief nervously in her hands. The pilot then gave a routine report of course and altitude, adding:

"Have just discovered we broke wheel in taking off—broke wheel in taking off. Stand by for a crash."

"A crash!" Miss Ball exclaimed, the color draining from her face. "Was that what he said?"

The operator stiffened as he heard the message. He reached for a telephone, and gave the report to an airport official. This man in turn directed that ambulance and fire-extinguishing equipment be sent on the field at once.

Kay and her mother escorted the distraught Miss Ball into the waiting room. Bill went outside.

"Clarence will be killed!" the actress muttered. "And it's all my fault. If I hadn't asked him to come here this wouldn't have happened!"

"Try to keep calm," Kay urged gently. "The pilot may very well be able to bring the plane down safely."

"With a wheel gone, there's nothing anyone can do to avert an accident," Miss Ball insisted. With this she got up and started pacing.

Mrs. Tracey and Kay exchanged knowing looks. It was clear to both of them that Miss Ball was in love with Clarence Minton. They did their best to comfort her, but she was too worried even to hear what they were saying, or notice when Bill came in.

"It's strange about the landing gear breaking," Kay said in an undertone to Bill. "Of course, accidents like that sometimes do occur—only——"

"It seems to have happened at a peculiar time, to say the least," Bill finished grimly.

"Do you think someone could have purposely damaged the plane? Someone who wanted to prevent Mr. Minton from coming here to help in the search for the kidnaper?"

"That may be a pretty shrewd guess. We have no way of knowing for sure, though," said Bill.

"If the plane was sabotaged by someone in New York, that would bear out my original idea," Kay said reflectively.

"Do you think the kidnaper is in league with some person connected with the theater or movie industry?"

"It's certainly a possibility."

Unknown to the Traceys, a newspaper reporter had observed them shortly after their arrival at the airport. Always on the alert for familiar faces, he had been quick to recognize Beatrice Ball, and had wondered what had brought her to the Carmont airport. Not wanting to miss a possible story, he asked for an interview.

"Oh, not now!" the actress protested. "I'm too upset."

The reporter, however, persisted and got her to tell of the situation with Minton's plane. After jotting down some notes, he dashed away but was back again in a few minutes. The news then spread about that a famous actress was in the waiting room and Miss Ball soon found herself surrounded by the curious.

"We must get away from here," Kay whispered to Bill.

They made a beeline for the doorway and escaped

into the night. A number of people however were milling about near the runway.

"The news has certainly spread rapidly," Mrs. Tracey said.

All of the lights bordering the runway had been turned on; several brilliant emergency beams were playing over the frozen ground where the crippled airplane was expected to land. When Miss Ball saw the fire engine and ambulance draw up near by, she shivered.

"If anything happens to Clarence, I'll never forgive myself. Never!" she said, her lips almost white.

"You must be brave, whatever happens," Kay whispered.

She had been watching the dark sky when suddenly she noticed a tiny red gleam. It seemed to be coming closer and closer.

"That must be the plane," she said quietly.

The crowd became more and more dense, until Kay and her companions had difficulty in maintaining their position in the front line of the runway.

As the plane was sighted, a tense silence fell over the crowd. All eyes were turned upward. A light beam played for an instant on the plane, and Kay was sure she saw one of the wheels dangling at a strange angle.

Twice the plane circled the airport as the pilot seemed to gather courage to make the descent. Then it slowly came down.

"Oh, I can't bear to look!" cried Miss Ball.

Kay felt the actress grip her hand so tightly that it hurt. All eyes were riveted on the plane. Would it crash?

IV

The Mysterious Stranger

The plane glided slowly downward. There was a slight shock as it struck the ground on its two good wheels, the right front and the rear.

A cheer of relief went up from the crowd, but the danger was not over. The plane rolled smoothly for a few yards, then skidded and flopped over on its left side.

"Oh no!" Miss Ball cried.

Policemen and field attendants held back the crowd but did allow the actress and her friends to go out on the field.

Kay and Miss Ball reached the plane just as the pilot and Clarence Minton stepped out of the cockpit, unhurt save for a few minor scratches. Both were smiling, though somewhat grimly.

Miss Ball rushed over to Minton, and eagerly caught his hand. "Oh, I'm so thankful you aren't hurt. When I heard about the damage I feared the worst!"

"We had a narrow escape," Minton admitted. "But thanks to my pilot here, we came through safe."

"That was a skillful landing," Miss Ball said to the pilot.

"We were awfully lucky."

The young woman chatted excitedly with her manager for several minutes, forgetting to introduce Kay, Mrs. Tracey, and Bill. With apologies the introductions were finally made.

Kay studied Clarence Minton with interest. She admired the calm way he talked about the accident. Although he was about forty years old, he looked much younger. His brown eyes seemed to soften as they rested upon Beatrice Ball. Kay guessed that his interest in the actress was not purely a professional one.

"Tell us how the wheel became loose," Miss Ball urged. "What caused it?"

The manager looked out over the crowd that was closing in upon them.

"We can't talk here," he answered quietly.

"You must both come with us," Mrs. Tracey insisted. "It is only a short drive to our home."

The little group, aided by a policeman, pushed their way through the crowd. Relieved to escape the reporters who had gathered to question the pilot, they hurried to Bill's car. Kay, unobserved by the others, suddenly halted.

Was it her imagination, or had she really seen who she thought she'd seen among the people? The familiar man wore a dark overcoat and a black hat pulled low over his eyes. He was watching Miss Ball intently.

Unexpectedly his gaze shifted, and his eyes met Kay's. She had not been mistaken. This was the same sinister looking man who had driven the tan car, which had probably hit Betty. Abruptly the man wheeled about and disappeared into the crowd.

"Bill!" Kay called sharply.

Then she saw that he was too far away to hear her. She hesitated only an instant before pursuing the stranger. She was afraid she had lost him completely, but a little later she noticed him far ahead of her, elbowing his way toward one of the hangars.

The man turned around and saw that Kay was following him. He broke into a run, and darted toward a small blue plane which had been warming up.

"Stop that man!" Kay cried frantically. "Stop him!"

Those who might have helped her seemed paralyzed for the moment. As the stranger flung himself into the cockpit, a mechanic raced toward him, but got there too late to prevent him from taking off.

The tail of the plane swung around, narrowly missing Kay and the mechanic. Both were sprayed with a fine slush of ice and snow, churned up behind the wheels.

As he opened the throttle wide, the stranger waved his hand mockingly and taxied across the field. He took off at a reckless angle, and ascended into a dark sky.

"Do you know who that was?" Kay asked the mechanic.

"Never saw him before. But he's stolen one of our best little planes!"

Then he hurried away to report the theft to the authorities. Kay went to the car and told everyone what had just happened.

"You're certain he was the man?" Bill questioned.

"Yes, I'm sure of it. I got only a glimpse of his face, but from his general appearance I easily recognized him."

"Is he tall?" Miss Ball asked.

"Yes, and quite thin. He walks with a jerky stride."

"Then he was the one who kidnaped me!"

During the ride back to Brantwood Mr. Minton filled everyone in on what had happened since he'd left New York. During the take-off he and the pilot had felt a slight jar, but had not suspected anything was wrong until they received a radio warning from the home airport. Since the message had not been relayed until they were well on their way, it had seemed to them wiser to continue on their course than to turn back.

"Do you think the broken wheel was the result of a natural accident?" Kay asked.

Minton hesitated before replying. Then he said tersely:

"The pilot thought the accident was premeditated. Tomorrow he intends to make a thorough examination of the plane to see what he can find."

"Did anyone know you were coming on this trip?" Kay asked.

"I've suspected for some weeks that something strange has been going on at my office. In several instances important information has leaked out."

"Do you think someone may have tried to prevent you from coming here tonight?"

"That thought occurred to me. But I can't imagine anyone having sufficient reason to plot against my life. That's what it comes to, of course. If it hadn't been for the skill of my pilot, I wouldn't be here now."

"Don't even talk about that," Miss Ball pleaded.

Minton squeezed her arm comfortingly, but said with determination:

"I intend to get to the bottom of this matter! I'll be more cautious in the future, but no one is going to intimidate me! If the plane was tampered with, it may very well have been done by someone who knew about Miss Ball's kidnaping and I'll do anything to learn his identity."

When they reached the Tracey home Kay showed Mr. Minton the ring and the glove.

"Have you ever seen either of them before?" Kay questioned.

"Not to my recollection. The ring is certainly unusual."

"You don't recall any man with six fingers?" Kay asked hopefully.

Minton shook his head.

Kay was disappointed but neither she nor Minton was willing to admit defeat.

"We'll continue this discussion in the morning," he promised. "My mind will be fresh then, and I may be able to dig up some clue which will be useful."

Miss Ball and her manager gratefully accepted Mrs. Tracey's hospitality. They were both so exhausted from their harrowing experiences that in the morning Mrs. Tracey did not wake them for breakfast. They were still sleeping at eleven o'clock.

"What about our trip to Aunt Jane's?" Kay asked her mother anxiously.

Kay did not want to leave the actress and her manager with the mystery unsolved. On the other hand, she did not want to miss the holidays at the home of her mother's favorite aunt. There would be good sledding and good skiing but the Thanksgiving feast would be the high point of the week.

"I wish Miss Ball and Mr. Minton could go with us to Aunt Jane's," Kay said impulsively to her mother. "Do you think Aunt Jane would mind?"

"Probably not, Kay. She loves having guests. But Miss Ball and her manager probably have other plans for the holidays."

"I suppose so," Kay sighed.

By lunch time the actress and her manager were up and looking greatly refreshed after their long rest.

"You've all been so good to me," Miss Ball said gratefully. "But I've imposed long enough."

"I want her to go into hiding until we've been able to trace the kidnaper," Minton declared.

"And I know just the place!" Kay exclaimed.

She told them about the proposed trip to Aunt Jane's, explaining that the elderly lady had a number of servants and a large house in a secluded neighborhood.

"You'll be perfectly safe with Auntie," Kay insisted.

"Why not go?" Mr. Minton urged. "It would be a nice change for you."

"I'd love to," Miss Ball said softly. "I haven't had an old-fashioned Thanksgiving in years. But I don't want to intrude."

"Aunt Jane will be delighted to have you," Kay insisted.

Kay ran off to phone her aunt. She explained the situation to her as best she could, but Aunt Jane was slightly deaf, and could not make out all that Kay said. She was particularly bewildered by the girl's mention of a six-fingered glove.

"I don't know what you're talking about," she declared. "When you come to see me I want you to leave your mysteries at home."

"Then you don't want me to bring any guests?" Kay chuckled.

"Guests!" Aunt Jane snapped. "Who was talking about guests? Of course I want you to bring them."

"How many?"

"The more the better," Aunt Jane assured her. "Bring Miss Ball and Mr. Mint."

"Minton," Kay corrected.

"Well, whatever his name is, bring him. And the Worth girls."

"Oh, that'd be wonderful!" Kay exclaimed. "I'm sure they'll come."

"There's just one condition," Aunt Jane announced. "If you want any turkey dinner at *my* house, leave that six-fingered glove at home!"

V

Chris Eaton's Hoax

Kay ran back to the dining room to assure Miss Ball and Clarence Minton that Aunt Jane had extended a cordial invitation to them to spend the Thanksgiving holidays at her home. Minton was very pleased that he had been included and accepted eagerly, as did Miss Ball.

"I'm afraid I have nothing to wear but the dress I have on," Miss Ball mentioned. "My clothes were in suitcases in my car."

"By the way," asked Kay, "where do you suppose your chauffeur and the car are now?"

Miss Ball shrugged her shoulders. She had tried to find him, and realized he was probably looking for her. She was sure, however, that eventually he'd return to New York, where she lived.

"I could have my maid send me some clothes," said the actress, "but there are some things I'll need for the country that I just don't have. I'd like to go skating and sledding and do all the things I've never had time for since I began my career."

"You'll have time to buy anything you need before we go. Unfortunately, I have another day of school before vacation."

"Do you think it's wise for Miss Ball to be seen on the street?" Minton asked doubtfully. "It seems to me she should remain hidden for a few days at least. That fiend may return and who knows what he might try."

"You're right," Kay agreed. "We're about the same height and weight, Miss Ball. I could buy whatever you need, and if it fits me it will probably fit you."

"It's nice of you to go to so much trouble for me," the actress said gratefully. "I'll make out a list of things I want."

While Miss Ball was doing this, Kay hurried to the Worth home to tell the girls the plans for the holidays.

"Kay, do you know it's all over town that Beatrice Ball is staying with you?" Wendy said, as Kay walked in.

"I wonder how it got out."

"I have no idea, but it was all over school this morning. Why weren't you there?"

"Because I was at the airport half the night, and Mother thought I needed the rest."

Kay told the girls about Aunt Jane's invitation. Betty and Wendy were eager to go, and their mother gave her consent. As Kay turned to leave the house, Betty called after her:

"Have any reporters tried to interview you?"

"Not yet," Kay answered. "I guess they haven't found us."

She was quite mistaken, however. At that very moment a group of newspapermen had gathered in Bill's office, and were trying to learn from him details of the airplane crash and the reason for Miss Ball's stay in Brantwood. But Bill managed to convince them that he had very little information.

"It's just as well that you are all leaving town tomorrow," he remarked that night at the Tracey dinner table. "I doubt that I'll be able to keep this pack of newspaper wolves at bay much longer."

"I wish you could go with us out to Aunt Jane's," Kay said wistfully.

"So do I, but I have important legal matters to attend to. I'll certainly be there for Thanksgiving day."

According to the plan, the little group was to leave for Aunt Jane's as soon as school was out on the following day.

"I'd love to take the glove and ring with me to Aunt Jane's," Kay thought mischievously. "I wonder if I should?"

She had carefully placed the objects in a bureau drawer, and then hurried off to school. She intended to mention the matter to Miss Ball when she returned that evening.

Kay had been so engrossed with the events of the past forty-eight hours, that she hadn't noticed Chris Eaton trying to get her attention in class.

During the break the usually unfriendly girl came over to Kay and offered her a chocolate, which she promptly refused.

"I wonder what's gotten into Chris?" Kay thought. "I'm sure it isn't the holiday spirit!"

Shortly afterward Chris Eaton revealed her motive by asking questions about Miss Ball.

"Is she really staying at your house?" she asked.

"She was our guest for the night," Kay answered tersely.

She quickly walked away before Chris could ask another question. When Wendy and Betty came over, she said to them in an undertone:

"Chris knows about Miss Ball. Whatever you do, don't let her suspect that she's still at my house."

"Sh!" Wendy hissed.

Kay wheeled about to find Chris standing close by. It was obvious she'd been eavesdropping.

"I hope she didn't hear us," Kay said uneasily.

"I have a feeling she did," Betty answered. "I saw her smirking to herself as she walked away."

The moment school was dismissed Kay hurried over to Bresham's Department Store, where she was to meet her mother. Miss Ball's shopping list was not a long one, and they were able to buy everything in less than an hour.

"I hope Miss Ball hasn't been lonesome during our absence," Kay commented as the two left the store.

"Mr. Minton is with her," her mother smiled. "He should make a far better companion than I."

Neither of them had the slightest suspicion that Miss Ball was at the moment alone in the house. Shortly after Mrs. Tracey's departure Mr. Minton had gone to the airport to talk to the pilot who had flown him to Carmont.

Miss Ball was reading a magazine, when the telephone rang. At first she didn't answer it, but when it continued ringing she picked it up. As she did so, a female voice called out:

"Hello. May I speak to Miss Ball?"

The actress hesitated slightly before admitting who she was. After she had done so, the person calling said:

"This is Miss Eaton—Miss Chris Eaton. I'm a very dear friend of Kay Tracey's. She asked me to call you."

"Oh," Miss Ball murmured in relief. "Did Kay give you a message for me?"

"Yes, she wants you to come to my house as soon as you can."

"But I don't understand——"

The actress was bewildered. Kay knew that Miss Ball was not to leave the house without an escort. She wondered if an emergency of some kind had arisen.

"I suppose I could take a taxi—" she began doubtfully.

"Yes, do," Chris purred. "We'll be waiting for you."

"I'll call back in a few minutes," Miss Ball said hastily, and hung up the receiver.

For an instant she stood by the telephone, wondering just what to do. She wished Clarence were there. If she waited a little while longer he might return. Meanwhile she checked the phone book for the Eaton address, underlining it with a pencil.

Several minutes elapsed, but Minton did not return. Finally, when she thought she could wait no longer, the actress called a cab. Then she opened the telephone book at Chris's address, with the intention of phoning the girl, as she had promised. But at that moment, her cab arrived and she hurried out of the house.

Ten minutes after Miss Ball left, Kay and her mother returned home. They were mystified to find the house deserted.

"It's very strange. I wonder where she is?" she commented uneasily.

"It worries me," Mrs. Tracey confessed.

Kay's eye suddenly fell upon the open telephone book. She looked at it and instantly saw that Chris Eaton's address had been underlined. Remembering the girl's interest in the actress, she suspected a scheme of some kind.

"I think I have a clue!" she cried, showing her mother the book. "I'm going over to Chris's this very minute!"

She ran outside, and jumped into the car.

"If Chris has tricked Miss Ball into coming to her house, I'll be furious with that girl!" she stormed.

Kay came within view of Chris's and instantly her fears were confirmed. A yellow taxi was standing at the curb. Two people were talking on the front steps, and as she drew closer, Kay recognized Chris and Miss Ball. They were having a heated argument.

"You called me here on the pretext that Kay wanted to see me!" Miss Ball exclaimed. "It was nothing but a trick!"

Chris looked embarrassed. She had naively expected that when Miss Ball reached her house it would be an easy matter to get her autograph and perhaps even persuade her to leave the Tracey home for the Eaton home.

"All I know is that Kay told me to tell you to come here," she muttered.

"I don't believe she ever made such a request."

Chris was about to break down and admit the trick she had played, when she saw Kay's car at the curb. She was momentarily confused. Then she decided to make another attempt to squirm out of the situation.

"Yes, Kay did ask me to make the call," she insisted. "And here she comes now, just as I told you she would!"

VI

Duplicity Exposed

"That isn't true, Chris!" Kay exclaimed, hurrying up the walk. "I heard what you just said."

Chris's face flushed. Then she turned on Kay furiously.

"You always come nosing in where you're not wanted!" she snapped. "Why don't you mind your own business?"

"This is very much my business, Chris. You had no right to ask Miss Ball to come here and then say that I had asked you to do it!"

"Oh, you disgust me, always trying to tell people what they should do and what they shouldn't! You want to keep Miss Ball to yourself for the publicity."

"I think Miss Eaton has just given her *own* reason for inviting me here," the actress said coldly. "Come on, Kay, let's go."

Arm in arm the two turned their backs on Chris and walked to Kay's car.

"I should have known it was a trick," Miss Ball said as they drove away. "What an unpleasant girl!"

"She's just suffering from an inflated ego," Kay said. "And she's always had too much money to spend."

"I shouldn't have left your house, yet I honestly

didn't know what to do. I was afraid there was some emergency and that you really wanted me to come."

"It wasn't your fault."

"I was so determined to keep people from learning where I was staying."

"It's lucky we're leaving soon for Aunt Jane's."

The departure for the country had already been delayed, due to Chris's prank. Kay drove home as quickly as she could. Minton had returned in the meantime, and was deeply distressed over Miss Ball's absence. He, too, became indignant when he learned of the trick that had been played on her.

It was getting late, and Mrs. Tracey wanted to start the trip before nightfall. While she attended to some last-minute packing, Miss Ball tried on the clothes Kay had bought for her, and found everything to be fine.

"You have excellent taste," she said. Kay was delighted. She'd been afraid the actress might not like the things she and her mother had picked out.

Finally, when all the bags were packed in the trunk, Mrs. Tracey gave some last-minute instructions to Bill.

"Watch carefully that the water pipes don't freeze," she said, as her nephew tucked a blanket around her feet. "They're predicting a cold wave for next week."

"I'll keep tabs on everything," he promised.

"I really hate to leave you here alone."

The travelers stopped at the Worth house to pick up Wendy and Betty. The new car was a bit crowded, but no one really minded. Mr. Minton drove and Miss Ball and Kay sat in the front seat with him.

"By the way," Kay asked the manager as they reached the open country, "have you found out anything more about the airplane accident?"

"I was talking with my pilot this afternoon. He says

he has proof that someone deliberately removed a cotter pin from one of the wheels and tampered with the undercarriage. But I have no idea who it could have been."

Now that they were out in the fresh, country air and away from the city, Miss Ball was relaxing and grew more talkative.

"I'm really looking forward to an old-fashioned Thanksgiving," she murmured dreamily. "Everything is so beautiful, with the snow and icicles shining on the trees. I was born on a farm. This visit will be like going home again."

"I always think of you as a city person," Kay said.

"I had never even been to a city before I was sixteen," the actress went on. "My parents didn't have much money, and we all had to work very hard. Yet even as a child I loved the theater and felt I was destined to go on the stage.

"I was determined to get an education. Before I entered High School I saved every penny I possibly could. I sewed and I cooked. Finally I had enough money to take me to college, where I studied dramatic art."

"Was it hard to get parts?" Betty asked.

"No, in my senior year I was in a show that attracted the attention of a professional. He offered me a small salary to be his partner, and I accepted it. Later I regretted my decision, for Harry Purcell was an erratic and unpleasant man."

"Purcell was your partner?" Kay inquired, making a mental note of it.

"Yes. He was not dependable in the least. One night he would perform marvelously, the next he would ruin the show with his lack of interest and his wild antics. Once I almost lost a part because of him. Finally I couldn't stand it any longer, and I left him."

"Did he try to make trouble for you after that?" Kay asked.

"Oh, he often threatened me, but I paid no attention to him. I haven't seen him since the day we parted several years ago in a little town way out in Nebraska."

Kay had been listening to the story with growing interest. Impulsively she suggested the possibility that Harry Purcell had been responsible for the kidnaping.

"I doubt it," Miss Ball responded. "Harry was a weak character and I don't think he would have the courage to attempt anything like that. Besides, there were five fingers on each of his hands."

"It was just a thought," Kay said.

The story had impressed her, however, and she made a point to remember Harry Purcell's name.

"After I left his show, I had a hard time finding work," Miss Ball continued. "Finally Clarence took an interest and agreed to manage me. Ever since I have been steadily climbing upward. I owe everything to Clarence."

"Nonsense!" Minton broke in quickly. "It's merely that I recognize great talent when I see it. You still have the heights before you, Beatrice."

"I hope we'll reach them together."

The car wound its way through pleasant, snow-blanketed valleys and over low hills. Occasionally it would pass an old-fashioned sleigh dashing by with a merry jingle of bells. It was getting dark, when Kay suddenly noticed a small boy trudging along the road carrying a large object in his arms.

"Let's offer the boy a ride," she suggested.

They stopped the car, and were surprised to see that the lad was carrying a live turkey. As he turned his face questioningly toward them, they saw tears trickling down his cheeks.

"Why, what's the matter?" Kay cried, getting out of the car and hurrying to his side. "What's wrong? Wouldn't you like a ride to your home?"

"I'm not going home. I'm on my way to town."

"Then we'll take you there," Kay offered. She glanced with interest at the fat bird. "I suppose this is your Thanksgiving dinner?"

Her words threw the boy into a flood of fresh tears. He began to stroke the turkey's head affectionately.

"I wouldn't eat old Gobbler if I starved to death!" he proclaimed. "I wouldn't sell him, either, only my mother and sisters haven't enough food in the house."

"Where do you live?" Kay asked gently.

The boy told her, and she recalled that they had passed the place only a short distance back. It was an old farmhouse, very much run-down and badly in need of repairs. She learned that the boy's name was Jimmie, and that besides his parents he had three sisters and a baby brother. For many days there had been very little to eat in the house. In desperation the family had decided that Jimmie's pet turkey must be sold so they could buy other food.

"Wait here just a minute," Kay requested.

She darted back to the car and described the situation.

"Can't we do something for the boy?" Miss Ball asked.

"I was thinking it would be nice if we could take him to town and buy the family some food. Then Jimmie won't have to sell old Gobbler."

"A fine idea!" Mr. Minton declared heartily. "I'll gladly pay for it all."

"We all must have a share in it," Mrs. Tracey insisted.

The surprised Jimmie was bundled into the car

along with his turkey. At the next town the travelers drew up in front of a butcher-grocery store. There, with the little boy watching in bewilderment, they bought a huge amount of food. As a crowning gesture Mr. Minton presented the boy with a twenty-pound dressed turkey.

"Now Mr. Gobbler can live to a ripe old age, Jimmie," he chuckled. "Jump into the car, and we'll drive you home."

The side trip had taken considerable time, but no one regretted the delay. They were amply repaid when they saw the happy faces of Jimmie's mother and her little children.

"This will be our nicest Thanksgiving in years," the woman told them gratefully. "Bless you all for your kindness."

It was well after seven o'clock when the group pulled up to Aunt Jane's rambling old white house. A short, gray-haired little lady in black silk flung open the door.

"Well, well, I thought you would never arrive!" she laughed. "Come in, all of you."

"You shouldn't be outdoors wearing only a shawl, Aunt Jane," Kay chided her, giving her an affectionate squeeze. "Anything to eat in the house?"

"Oh, perhaps a few bones," the little old lady chuckled.

She greeted Miss Ball and Mr. Minton with such warmth they were at ease at once.

"Where is Bill?" she inquired indignantly. "If that scalawag has disappointed me—"

"He'll be here for Thanksgiving dinner," Kay told her. "Nothing in the world could make him miss that."

"Well, he'd better come!" Aunt Jane said, leading the way to the living room, where a fire blazed in the hearth.

A servant took the bags and led everyone to their rooms. Half an hour later a sumptuous supper was served in the dining room.

"I can't give you much tonight," Aunt Jane apologized. "I want to starve you all so you'll do justice to our big turkey! I bought a forty-pound one this year. Had to scour two counties to get it."

"You don't expect us to eat forty pounds of turkey!" Kay gasped.

"That's only five pounds apiece, not counting any for the servants," Aunt Jane retorted.

"If I eat five pounds of turkey I'll have to buy a new wardrobe," Wendy said.

After supper the girls went to their rooms to unpack. As Betty was pulling out her skating outfit, she noticed Kay lift a small black object from her purse, and slip it under a pillow on her bed.

"What was that?" Betty asked.

"Oh, just a little souvenir," she answered.

Betty pounced on the pillow, and before Kay could stop her, pulled out the mysterious object.

"The six-fingered glove!" she exclaimed. "Why did you bring that?"

Kay smiled as she picked it up and carefully put it away, together with the mysterious diamond ring she had found inside it.

"I just might have some use for these during my visit. You never know."

VII

A Valuable Clue

"Kay, you might as well show it to me," Aunt Jane commented shrewdly, as she and her niece sat chatting in the living room after everyone else in the house had retired.

"Show you what, Aunt Jane?" Kay asked innocently.

"Fiddlesticks! You needn't pretend you don't know what I mean. The glove, of course!"

"But you told me to leave it at home."

"I knew very well you wouldn't obey," the elderly lady chuckled. "What's that you were telling me about it having six fingers?"

"I'll show you, Aunt Jane."

Kay ran to her room to get the glove and the ring. She laid them both in her aunt's hand, then briefly outlined the story connected with them.

"Well, well," said Aunt Jane, "this is an odd case, to say the least."

"Did you ever hear of anyone with six fingers?" Kay asked.

"No, I can't say I ever did. But I suppose there are such people."

She turned the glove inside out to look for the manufacturer's name.

"It isn't there," Kay said. "I've already looked for it."

"You seem to think of everything," her Aunt Jane declared, a twinkle in her eyes.

"I wish I did. I'd sure like to find a way to track down that kidnaper!"

"You won't locate him here, I'm sure. I don't keep kidnapers on my premises."

"You may be surprised yet at what I'll find before I go home!" Kay threatened.

Aunt Jane glanced at the clock, and got up. It was long past her usual bedtime. She gave the glove and the ring back to Kay and together they climbed the stairs.

"We'll talk further about this tomorrow," she promised as they parted at Kay's door. "Pleasant dreams."

Aunt Jane was far too busy the following day supervising the preparations for Thanksgiving dinner to talk about the mystery. Kay and her friends discovered that the hills were in perfect condition for sledding and spent most of the day outside. Beatrice Ball said she hadn't enjoyed herself so much in years. She looked stunning in the clothes Kay had selected for her, and the girls noticed that Clarence Minton cast more than one admiring glance in her direction.

Late the next afternoon Bill arrived. Aunt Jane scurried about attending to last-minute details. The house was filled with the tantalizing aroma of mince pie baking.

"Isn't Thanksgiving ever coming?" Kay complained. "I can hardly wait, with all these wonderful smells floating around."

The holiday dawned clear and crisp, the ground covered with two feet of snow. Bill spent the morning shoveling a path around the house and out to the garage. He said he wanted to work up an appetite, though this was hardly necessary, as he always had a good one.

At one o'clock Aunt Jane summoned her guests to the great feast. The huge turkey, crisp and brown, rested on a platter in front of Bill's place. He carved quickly and skillfully, giving generous helpings to everyone, until he came to Kay. To tease her, he pretended he was going to give her the neck, a piece she hated.

During the meal the doorbell rang. A servant came to inform Aunt Jane that a group of reporters had arrived from the city.

"Reporters?" she repeated in annoyance. "Tell them to go away and let us eat our dinner in peace."

"Now, Aunt Jane, you just can't do that," Bill insisted. "Who do they want to see?"

"Miss Ball, sir," the servant answered.

"This is an outrage!" Minton said. "They've followed her here. If it gets generally known where she is staying, our plans will be ruined."

"Leave the reporters to me," Bill smiled. Turning to the servant, he said, "I'll see them as soon as I finish my dinner."

Although everyone tried to be cheerful and act as if nothing had happened, the interruption had been disturbing. Miss Ball looked slightly worried; Clarence Minton's scowl showed that he was still annoyed; Bill lapsed into a thoughtful silence.

"If I had my way I'd send those reporters packing!" Aunt Jane announced crossly.

Without meaning to do so, everyone hurried through their dessert. Bill then excused himself and went to talk to the reporters. Later, as Kay started for the second floor, she saw that the men were about to leave. One of them noticed her.

"Wait," he said unexpectedly, "I heard that a girl picked up a glove at the scene of the automobile accident. Was it you?"

"No," she replied. "By the way, did you ever hear of a man with six fingers?"

"What do you mean? Is this a joke?"

"I'm quite serious. I heard about such a case recently, and it just occurred to me that you reporters see a lot of unusual people. I thought possibly you might have met such a person."

"Not I!"

"Why, I once knew a man with six fingers," another newspaperman spoke up. "He was a strange guy—kept a fruit store in Collston."

"In Collston?" Kay repeated eagerly. "Do you remember his name?"

"It's Cortez, or something like that. Yes, I'm pretty sure it's Felix Cortez."

The man was on the verge of asking a question, when Bill interrupted:

"It's quite possible I'll have a really good story for you boys one of these days. If anything breaks, I'll remember you."

He escorted the reporters to the door. After it had closed behind them he turned to Kay with a smile of admiration.

"Nice work!"

"You took care of them," Kay laughed. "How far is Collston from here?"

"About forty miles."

"I could make it easily in a morning. I think I'll drive over there tomorrow and look for that six-fingered man. We may have found the person we're after."

"Don't you want me to go along?" Bill offered.

"No, it might arouse Cortez's suspicions if he is the

guilty party. I'll take Wendy and Betty with me."

Kay filled her friends in on the plan, and they were eager to go with her. They wanted to make the trip that very day, but realized that the fruit store would probably be closed.

Shortly after breakfast the next morning Kay and the twins set off for Collston. Although Bill had said it was only forty miles away, they soon discovered that they'd have to take a detour, which would make the trip much longer. The narrow, twisting road seemed endless but it finally emerged into a quaint little village.

"I wonder where we are?" said Wendy. "It reminds me of a town I once saw in a movie."

Kay's attention was drawn to the left-hand side of the highway. She pointed to a number of unusual looking objects which resembled signboards, yet obviously were not.

"What are they?" Betty asked.

Kay stopped the car, and she and her friends walked across the street to get a closer look.

"Why, they're movie props," Kay exclaimed. "See. That one seems to be the wall of a house; another represents an interior."

"But what are they doing here?" Wendy wondered.

Just then an elderly man came down the street wheeling a cart of potatoes. Kay asked him about the scenery.

"Lots of folks ask about this place," the old fellow chuckled. "These things belong to a movie company that worked here last summer."

After he had moved on the girls went over to the lot and looked around. They had just discovered a complete set-up of a cottage, when they heard heavy steps directly behind them. Turning around, they found themselves facing the watchman of the grounds.

"You can't p-p-play around here!" he stuttered, picking up a big stick. "G-go away! Be gone!"

"We're not doing any harm," Kay protested.

"You h-h-heard me. This is p-p-private property and no one is allowed to trespass. Hurry up, g-g-get moving!"

The three girls quickly retreated to the car, grumbling a little at such rude treatment. However, they had seen all they cared to and were ready to continue their trip.

A little later they drove into Collston and asked for directions to Felix Cortez's store.

"It's a dreadful looking place," Wendy said, viewing the store. "I wouldn't want to eat any of the fruit sold in there."

"Look!" Kay exclaimed.

She pointed to a car which was parked near the shop.

"That looks exactly like the car that hit me," Betty gasped.

"Maybe we've found our man," Kay declared. "Let's go inside and buy some fruit."

"First let's look in the window," Wendy suggested.

Unaware that their actions would arouse suspicion, the girls slowly sauntered down the street. When they reached the Cortez store they paused in front of the window. A man in a dirty white apron was weighing oranges for a customer.

"He's awful looking," Wendy whispered.

"And see, he *does* have an extra finger on one of his hands," Betty whispered.

"He's the one we want," Betty declared firmly. "Let's go in and question him."

VIII

The Spider

The three girls entered the fruit store, pretending to be interested in a box of strawberries. As they did so they cautiously scrutinized Cortez. They did not realize that he in turn was regarding them suspiciously.

Felix Cortez was even worse looking at close range. His face was deeply scarred, and his nose was severely misshapen.

"How much are your strawberries?" Kay asked, as Cortez approached her.

"Strawberries, Miss? Zey are high at zis time of year," he said as he pointed to his price chart.

While the girls pretended to study the chart Cortez stared at them closely. "Here are banana," he offered. "Zey are much cheap-air."

"And nearly spoiled, too," Betty added under her breath.

"You young ladies not from Collston?" the man asked abruptly.

"No," Wendy answered. "We live in Brantwood."

"Oh! Brantwood, eh? I drive zere few time—once try to collect bill."

"Is that your car outside?" Betty led him on. "The tan one?"

"Yes, eet ees mine," the man acknowledged. "Why you travel so far from home?"

"Oh, we're just out on a little jaunt," Kay answered.

"You very fond of high-price fruit. Perhaps you like zees fancy grape. Zey cost more zan anyzing in my store."

He reached up and lifted the fruit from a shelf. It was then that the girls got a good look at his six-fingered hand. Cortez's behavior struck Kay as odd and his last statement was particularly strange.

The girls decided to take a small bunch of the grapes. After weighing them Cortez announced the price, which was even higher than the girls had expected. Kay was about to pay when she realized she'd foolishly left the house without any money.

"I don't have a cent," she exclaimed. "Betty, can you pay?"

"Perhaps you would like to charge it!" Felix Cortez said with a curl of his lip.

"Why, that's very nice of you," Kay thanked him. "Especially when you don't know us."

"You make mistake. I know you very well. Excuse a moment, please."

He disappeared into a room at the rear of the store.

"What did he mean by that?" Betty asked, staring after him. "You don't think he suspects why we came here, do you?"

"It's possible," Kay said.

"Let's leave the fruit and get out of here," Wendy suggested. "He must be the man we're after. Let's get the police and have him arrested."

"We can't be too hasty," Kay answered. "We have to be absolutely certain he's the right person."

After a few minutes Cortez returned. In the meantime, Wendy and Betty had gotten together money for the grapes, but for some reason Cortez seemed far from eager to accept it. He kept looking for a better bunch of grapes and when he finally found one weighed it several times. Then he spent some time rummaging around for a bag. It was obvious the man was stalling.

In the meantime Kay tried to get some information out of him but all her questions were carefully evaded. He would not admit to being in Brantwood the night of the kidnaping, nor did a casual mention of Miss Ball's name produce the slightest flicker of interest in him. On the other hand he was trying to learn by various means the names of the girls and their addresses. Finally it became apparent to Kay that they just weren't getting anywhere with Cortez.

"We better be going now," she remarked, picking up the bag of grapes.

Cortez darted ahead of her and barred the door.

"Oh, no you don't!" he sneered. "You going to stay right here!"

"Move aside!" Kay ordered sharply. "You have no right to do this."

"I keep you 'til you pay bill you owe me!"

"You must be crazy!" Wendy cried indignantly. "We just paid you an exorbitant price for your grapes. They're not even fresh."

"How about all zat fruit I send you? Last week I send crate of oranges to three young lady in Brantwood. Two day ago you tell me send box of apple. Not one cent I get in pay."

"We don't know anything about any fruit," Kay insisted.

"No, and what's more, I don't believe you delivered fruit to anyone!" Betty cried indignantly. "You're the man who hit me and drove off without even stopping to see if I had been hurt."

"You kidnaped Miss Ball!" Wendy accused.

The fruit dealer began to wring his hands in distress and anger. Lapsing into his native tongue, he poured out a torrent of bitter words. In the midst of the commotion a policeman entered the store.

"What's going on here?" the officer demanded. "Are these the young women you reported to me, Cortez?"

"Yes, yes," the man nodded eagerly. "Arrest zem! Zey cheat me of a lot of money."

"That isn't true," Kay protested.

She now knew why Felix Cortez had spent so much time weighing the fruit and making the sale. Under the pretext of finding a bag he had gone to the rear of the store to phone the police, and had tried to kill time so the girls wouldn't leave before the officer arrived.

"He's the one who should be arrested!" Betty told the policeman furiously. "He is a hit-and-run driver."

"I think this is a case of mistaken identity," Kay said, speaking calmly. "I doubt that Mr. Cortez even knows our names."

"Oh, don't I?" the man retorted. "You are ze Winton sisters."

"The what sisters?" Wendy cried. "Who are they? A singing group?"

"You won't be zo funny when you go to ze jail," Cortez snarled. "Arrest zese young lady, officer."

"Not so fast, Cortez," the policeman said. "I want to get to the bottom of this."

By this time a number of people had gathered outside the store, trying to find out what was going on inside.

"Let's talk this over in the storage room," said the officer.

Kay and her friends were willing to comply,

confident that they could establish their true identity. Wendy and Betty were certain that Cortez had made the false accusation to distract attention from the kidnaping. Kay, however, tended to think that he actually had been cheated by three young women.

"We are not the Winton sisters," Kay insisted. "My friends are Betty and Wendy Worth and my name is Kay Tracey."

"Any relation to Bill Tracey?" the officer inquired.

"He is my cousin."

"You don't say? Well, Cortez, you've made a bad mistake, all right. This young lady is known as an amateur detective. She's done work that would be a credit to a professional!"

"It was a mystery that brought her here today!" Betty said before Kay could speak. "We think this man is involved in a kidnaping!"

"What proof do you have?" Cortez demanded hoarsely.

"Your hand! You have an extra finger on it. The night of the kidnaping Beatrice Ball snatched a glove with six fingers from you."

"Just a minute," said Kay, placing a quieting hand on Betty's arm. "Mr. Cortez may be right after all."

"He may be right! How can you say that, Kay?" Wendy and Betty were thoroughly bewildered.

"Didn't Miss Ball snatch a right-handed glove from the kidnaper?"

"Yes," said Betty.

"Mr. Cortez's extra finger is on his *left* hand."

"Zat ees true," the fruit dealer affirmed, holding out his left hand for the girls' inspection. After one hasty glance they averted their eyes.

"It looks as if I'm not needed here any longer," the policeman declared. "These young ladies didn't steal the fruit and you couldn't have been responsible for the kidnaping. It was just an unfortunate misunderstanding, nothing more."

As the officer turned toward the door he accidentally bumped into some bananas that had been partially unpacked. As they toppled toward the floor, he reached out a hand to check the fall.

"Look out!" Kay screamed.

The warning came too late. A dark, hairy, spider-like creature hurled itself upward from the fruit and struck the officer's hand. He gave a cry of pain as he brushed the bug to the floor.

"A tarantula!" Kay cried in horror, crushing it beneath her foot. "Its bite is poisonous!"

As the others stood by, dazed, and not knowing what to do, Kay hurried the policeman to her car. Betty and Wendy followed, and they drove as rapidly as they could to the nearest hospital, the officer directing them. Although his face was pale he made no complaint, but sat holding his wrist tightly with his uninjured hand.

They rushed him into the hospital's emergency room. After a while a white clad attendant came to tell them that because they'd acted so fast the policeman would be all right.

"Well, I'm glad we were able to do some good, even if this trip failed as far as our main purpose was concerned," Kay remarked. "We'd better get back to Aunt Jane's."

Approaching the hospital lobby, the girls noticed three policemen. They would have walked right on by had not one of the men caught Kay firmly by the shoulder.

"Not so fast, kid," he snapped. "You won't find it so easy to escape us this time!"

IX

Timely Assistance

"What's going on?" the girls asked.

It turned out that Felix Cortez's earlier phone call to police headquarters was the cause of all the trouble. When the officer who had been sent to the store failed to make a routine check-in, other policemen were sent to the scene. One of the onlookers told them the three girls had driven off in the direction of the city hospital.

The policemen followed the car to the hospital, assuming that the girls had in some way eluded the officer originally sent to arrest them. As the girls were trying to explain the situation, the policeman they had helped entered the lobby, his hand neatly bandaged.

"Hello, boys," he greeted his fellow officers with a smile. "I just had a little accident. Thanks to these girls, I'm still alive."

He explained how Kay and her friends had rushed him to the hospital, and completely exonerated them from the charge made against them by Felix Cortez. While the policemen were discussing the matter, they were joined by the doctor who had dressed the man's wound.

"I must ask you to lower your voices," he requested politely. "Sound carries very clearly in these halls."

The officers hastily apologized and headed for the door. Kay and her friends followed, but the doctor detained them.

"Aren't you the young lady who brought Officer Phillips to the hospital?" he asked Kay.

"Yes," she acknowledged. "I'm glad he's all right."

"He was very lucky. If the poison had spread through his system, he would have been in very serious trouble."

They chatted a few minutes longer. It seemed to Betty and Wendy that Kay was prolonging the conversation.

"Doctor, do you know of cases where people were born with six fingers on one hand?" she asked.

"Why, yes. We have an example of it right here in our city; a fruit dealer."

"I've already met him," Kay smiled. "Do you know of any other instances?"

"Several of them. As a matter of fact one was reported in my medical journal only last month. Such cases occasionally come my way, although they're rare. Why are you so interested, may I ask?"

"Just curiosity, I guess. I found a six-fingered glove, and it started me thinking."

"I'll bet you read a lot of mysteries," the doctor observed, a twinkle in his eye.

"I do."

"I'll tell you a little secret. I write them myself."

"How interesting!" Kay exclaimed.

"Of course, it's just a hobby. After a nerve-racking day at the clinic I find writing very relaxing."

"Do you find it difficult to come up with good plots?" Kay asked.

"Not particularly. I usually choose something with a scientific background. When you mentioned a six-fingered glove it made me think of my latest story. One of the characters has an extra finger on one of his hands. A couple of years ago I sold the story to a movie company."

"Has the movie been made yet?" Wendy asked.

"Yes," the doctor answered with pride. "The Eagle Film Company made the picture this past summer. Many of the scenes were shot at a little village only a few miles from here so I was able to watch some of the work. They even found an actor with six fingers on one hand."

Before the girls could ask the name of the picture, a nurse came to tell the doctor that he was needed immediately in the children's ward. He excused himself and hurried away.

"I guess we've seen the place where the doctor's movie was filmed," Kay said, as the girls turned to leave the hospital. "It must have been on the very lot where the watchman drove us away."

"I wish we'd gotten the name of the movie," Wendy commented. "I'd like to see it when it's released."

As they emerged from the hospital, the girls were surprised to find it snowing again. Big flakes were driven against their faces by a strong north wind, and the temperature had dropped.

"We've got to get home," Kay said uneasily. "If this keeps up the roads will quickly get very bad."

She had good reason to be worried about the drive back. The cold weather had followed a thaw, and the pavement was now covered with ice. The windshield of the car became so encrusted with snow, the wiper couldn't remove it.

When they arrived on the outskirts of the city Kay got out to clean the windshield with a salt solution, but it quickly coated over again.

"This is terrible," Betty said nervously. "It'll take hours to get back to your Aunt's."

"If we ever get there," Kay added grimly.

It required intense concentration to drive in this weather. The wind had caused the snow to drift and in many places it was difficult to tell where the road left off and the ditch began. In other spots the road was frozen over with a dangerous coating of ice.

They passed the village where they had seen the movie sets, but were so intent trying to follow the road that they gave the grounds on either side little more than a casual glance.

Kay inched along for several miles. Then, approaching a steep hill, she picked up speed. As they reached the top another car loomed up directly in their path. To avoid a crash Kay slammed on the brakes. Her car skidded sideways in the road and slid into the ditch.

"Now we've done it," she said, after making sure that neither Wendy nor Betty had been hurt.

Climbing out of the car, the girls discovered that the wheels on the right side were buried deep in the snow. The driver of the other car had stopped a little farther up the road and now came to see if he could be of any assistance.

"I'll definitely need some help," Kay admitted.

Kay climbed back into the car and started the motor but the wheels just spun around in the snow.

"I'll tow you," the stranger offered. "I have a rope with me."

He hitched on, and after two unsuccessful attempts finally pulled the car back onto the road. Kay thanked the man and offered to pay him for his trouble, but he would accept nothing.

"The accident was partly my fault," he stated. "The snow blinded me and I took up too much of the road."

Kay thanked the man and the girls continued toward their destination. The storm seemed to be getting worse by the minute. As far as the eye could see, the landscape was covered by a deep blanket of snow; the car looked as if it had been dipped in fluffy white icing.

"They'll all be so worried about us," Kay said anxiously. "I'd hurry, only it wouldn't be safe."

Kay switched on the headlights, but the beam made only a slight impression against the cloud of descending snowflakes.

"It feels like we've traveled a hundred miles since we left Collston."

As the car went round a bend Kay almost came to a stop.

"What's the matter?" asked Wendy.

"I thought I heard a train."

"I didn't hear anything. Did you, Betty?"

"No, but I see a railroad crossing signal straight ahead."

Kay stopped the car a short distance from the tracks.

"The light isn't flashing. I must have imagined that train whistle."

"I remember this place," said Wendy. "It doesn't have a signal."

"That's right," Betty agreed. "It has a tower and a watchman, who operates the gates."

"Well, they're apparently up now, so I guess it's all right for us to drive across," Wendy added.

As she spoke, they heard the long, shrill blast of a train.

"That must be the late afternoon express," Betty murmured. "It's lucky you stopped, Kay. The gates must not be working."

At that moment the girls saw an old watchman run frantically from the tower and towards the safety gates. A car was slowly approaching on the opposite side of the tracks. The old man tugged desperately at the barriers, trying to draw them into position.

"He needs help!" Kay cried, jumping out of the car. "If the gates aren't down those people could be killed!"

X

An Alarming Discovery

The girls raced through the blinding snow to the railroad tracks. Betty used her red scarf to flag the oncoming car, while Kay and Wendy helped the old watchman pull the barriers into place.

At first the bars wouldn't budge, but with the three of them pulling as hard as they could the gates finally swung down. Seconds later the express thundered by, its windows agleam with lights.

The approaching car had stopped abruptly. Another car coming from the opposite direction, which the girls hadn't noticed, also came to a standstill.

"That's the first time them gates ever jammed," the old watchman gasped. "If you girls hadn't 'a helped me I never could 'a got the bars down in time!"

When the train had disappeared in the distance, the girls helped the man raise the barriers so the cars could continue on their way.

"I'll have to send for help," said the watchman. "With these bars out o' order the crossin' ain't safe."

As the girls stood shivering in the cold, wondering whether they should offer to stay with the watchman until help arrived, a boy of about twenty appeared with a tin dinner pail.

"Here's your supper, Pop," he said, holding out the bucket. "Mother sent an extra cup of hot coffee tonight because it's so cold."

"This is my son Albert," the old man said, relieved. "He can help me with the bars until the machinery's fixed. The next train ain't due for an hour, anyway.

"These girls saved some lives tonight," the watchman explained to his son. "That car never would 'a stopped if the bars hadn't 'a come down when they did."

With that the girls said good-bye and hurried back to their car at the side of the road. They still had quite a ways to go and it was growing darker.

"It's only a little after five," Betty said, looking at her watch, "but it seems much later."

They managed to cover the remaining distance without mishap. Great was their joy and relief when they saw Aunt Jane's house looming up on the hilltop. As they drove into the grounds, Bill came out to meet them.

"I'll put the car away," he offered. "Run into the house and warm up. Kay, your mother has been terribly worried."

"We did have several accidents," she laughed. "But fortunately nothing really disastrous happened."

Mrs. Tracey and Aunt Jane were waiting for them in the hall. They helped the girls remove their coats, and made them warm themselves by the fire. While Kay restored the circulation to her almost frozen hands, she relayed all that had happened since they'd left the house.

"I'm afraid you're almost too kind-hearted for your own good, Kay," Mrs. Tracey chided. "Some day you may find yourself in a serious predicament."

"Well, as long as she knows how to get out of it, she'll be all right," Aunt Jane chuckled.

The old lady gave Kay's cheek an affectionate pinch as she went to the kitchen to order an especially good supper for the girls.

"Where are Miss Ball and Mr. Minton?" Kay asked her mother when they were alone in the living room.

"Oh, they went for a little walk."

"A walk! In this blizzard?"

"Well, love doesn't pay attention to weather!" laughed Mrs. Tracey.

"Do you think they're really in love, Mother?"

"Clarence Minton worships Beatrice, Kay. It is very apparent."

"But I wonder if she feels the same way about him?"

"I haven't made up my mind about that. Sometimes I doubt if Beatrice really knows herself how she feels."

"They make a good couple," Kay said with a sigh. "I think they should get married."

"Well, don't try to arrange that," Mrs. Tracey said, laughing.

Late that evening, after everyone but Kay and Miss Ball had retired, Miss Ball started to talk about Clarence Minton.

"Do you really like him, Kay?" she asked.

"Very much."

"Some months ago he asked me to marry him but I refused."

Kay made no comment, but tried to hide her disappointment.

"Clarence is one of my dearest friends, and at times I feel sure that I love him. However, when he asked me to be his wife I said that I could not say yes until he had fulfilled a certain ideal of mine."

Kay was dying to ask what that might be, but tactfully refrained from doing so.

"Now he has done that, and I must give him my answer," the actress went on. "I don't know what to tell him."

"I'm afraid I can't advise you," Kay smiled. "Mr. Minton seems to be a fine man, but I don't really know him."

"He *is* fine, Kay. I've never met anyone more honest or kind. He's always been devoted to me and my interests."

"Are you afraid you don't love him? Is that it?"

"I think I love him," Miss Ball answered. "Until we came here together I wasn't sure. But being with him in this beautiful spot has changed my outlook. I really think that my answer will be 'yes.'"

"I hope you'll both be very happy," said Kay fervently.

The next day Mr. Minton and Miss Ball were together almost constantly. They went for a long walk in the woods and spent the afternoon skating on a nearby pond. Knowing they wanted to be alone, Kay and the twins discreetly kept their distance. As the evening wore on it became evident from Minton's tense manner that he had not yet received an answer from Miss Ball.

"Why doesn't she just say 'yes' if she's going to?" Kay said to her friends. "If I ever get married, I'll certainly make up my mind about it without so much delay."

"I'm sure Ronald Earle will be delighted to hear that!" Betty teased.

"Ronald Earle!" Kay exclaimed, blushing. "He's just a friend, nothing more!"

"His status may change in later years," Betty giggled.

"Let's not talk about love any more," Kay said. "I've heard enough about it for one day."

That evening both Mr. Minton and Miss Ball were strangely quiet at dinner; yet a warm light shone in the actress's eyes, and everyone guessed that she intended to give Mr. Minton her answer very soon. When the meal was over Aunt Jane retired to her own quarters. Mrs. Tracey followed a little later. Bill pretended to be very tired. Kay, Wendy, and Betty soon found an excuse for leaving the living room.

"Well, if Miss Ball doesn't say 'yes' now, it isn't because she hasn't had a chance!" Betty chuckled. "What shall we do with ourselves all evening?"

"I'm going to read some poetry," Wendy announced, taking a book from her suitcase.

Betty decided to do some knitting. She was making a sweater for her mother as a Christmas gift, but during the past few weeks had not accomplished very much. Kay glanced at the evening newspaper, then tossed it aside.

"I guess I'll take another look at my six-fingered glove," she said, a twinkle in her eyes.

"I wish you'd left that thing at home!" Wendy said, looking up from her book. "It gives me the creeps."

Kay went to her suitcase and took out the glove. As she ran her hand down into it she uttered a faint cry.

"The diamond ring! It's gone!" she gasped.

"Gone?" Betty exclaimed. "Where did you keep it?"

"Why, right where I found it—in a finger of the glove."

"Then it must be there."

"It isn't. It's gone!"

"Maybe it dropped down into your suitcase," Wendy said, getting up to help look for it. "I'll find it for you."

She shook out all the clothes in the suitcase, but the ring was not there.

"You're sure you put the ring in the glove?" Betty asked.

"Yes, I distinctly remember doing so," Kay cried in distress.

"I wonder what happened to it," Betty said in bewilderment.

"Someone must have stolen it!"

The girls ran off to tell Mrs. Tracey and Aunt Jane what had happened. Aunt Jane was particularly disturbed by the strange disappearance, and immediately called her housekeeper. However, that woman could shed no light on the mystery, insisting that all her servants were honest.

"I've had them with me for years," Aunt Jane stated. "I don't believe anyone in my house would steal anything."

"I'm going to tell Miss Ball!" Kay cried. "The ring was as much hers as it was mine."

The three girls rushed down to the living room, bursting in on Clarence Minton and the actress just as the man was placing a beautiful diamond engagement ring on the young woman's finger. Betty, who was the last to enter, didn't think before she spoke.

"The ring's been stolen!" she blurted out. Springing to her feet Miss Ball gazed in bewilderment at the glittering diamond on her own finger. Her face turned white.

"Stolen!" she gasped. "This ring stolen?"

Then she fainted.

XI

An Embarrassing Mistake

Minton caught the actress as she crumpled to the floor. With Kay's help he lifted her to a sofa. His face was white with anger at Betty's thoughtlessness and he would not even look at her.

"I'm terribly sorry," Betty murmured. "I didn't mean it the way it sounded. I had no idea——"

"You've ruined everything for me," Minton said gruffly.

Anxiously Minton tried to revive the unconscious actress. Kay ran to the kitchen for a glass of water, but when she returned the young woman had come to.

"My ring—stolen," she whispered. "I can't believe it."

"It was all a mistake," Kay comforted her. "Betty didn't mean your ring—she meant the diamond we found in the six-fingered glove. It was thoughtless and rude of us to break in on you the way we did. We were upset about losing the diamond, and didn't stop to think about what we said or did."

"I can't tell you how sorry I am," Betty said earnestly. "I hope you'll forgive me."

"Of course, Betty, there's really nothing to forgive."

Nevertheless, the girls realized that their thought-lessness had spoiled what otherwise would have been a very special moment for Miss Ball.

"I'm sorry I spoke so sharply to you," Minton told Betty regretfully.

"I deserved it," Betty responded.

"I hope the engagement is still on," Wendy remarked when the girls were upstairs.

There was a light tap on the door. Kay quickly went to answer it.

"Can I talk to you for a moment outside?" Miss Ball asked.

Kay nodded and stepped into the hall, closing the door behind her. She noticed at once that the diamond was no longer on the actress's finger.

"It's about Clarence," Miss Ball said hurriedly. "He's leaving."

"Leaving? Not tonight?"

"Yes, I returned his ring, and it hurt him dread-fully. He's in his room now, packing."

"You don't want him to go?" Kay asked.

"No, I care about him more than I realized."

Kay considered the actress somewhat flighty in her feelings, but she wisely refrained from saying so. Instead, she asked, "If you love him, why don't you keep the ring?"

"I don't know. I was so upset and confused. I wish now that I had accepted it, but it's too late. He's leaving."

"I'll take care of that," Kay promised with a smile. "You go wait in the living room."

The actress had just disappeared down the stairway when Minton's bedroom door opened. He stepped out into the hall, carrying a suitcase in one hand.

"Please give my regrets to your mother," he said, addressing Kay stiffly. "I'm afraid that I must return to the city at once."

"If you do, it will be the biggest mistake of your life."

"What do you mean?"

"Miss Ball is deeply in love with you."

Minton laughed bitterly, and took from his vest pocket the diamond ring which had been returned to him. "This doesn't look much like it!"

"She's been under a terrific nervous strain the past week—ever since the kidnaping," Kay said quietly. "Tonight she was understandably upset by what Betty said. I suspect she's regretting her behavior this very minute. Why don't you go down to the living room and talk to her again?"

"Do you think it would do any good?" he asked eagerly.

"I'm sure it would."

Full of new hope Minton hurried down the stairway.

"Well, that's fixed up," Kay sighed confidently. "Now I can start thinking about my own ring. But it's so late I guess nothing more can be done until morning."

Before she retired she spoke again to her mother and Aunt Jane. Both were distressed about the ring and promised that a thorough search would be made in the morning.

"I'll have the bedroom carefully swept," Aunt Jane declared. "Perhaps we'll find it."

At breakfast the next day the smiling Miss Ball was again wearing Minton's ring.

"I'm deeply indebted to you for all you've done," she whispered to Kay. "I want you to be maid of honor at my wedding."

"I'd love to," Kay replied.

No further mention was made of the lost ring, but after breakfast a thorough search was begun. The bedroom was gone over very carefully a second time, but the ring was nowhere to be found.

"I hate to say it," Kay said to Aunt Jane, "but I'm afraid someone in this house is a thief."

"I've been trying to figure out who that might be," the old lady returned. "All my servants have been with me so many years that I trust them implicitly. I do have one new employee working for me, but he seldom comes into the house."

"What's his name, Aunt Jane?"

"Ike Stone. He looks after the horses and tends to the garden during the summer. I hired him a few months ago but have been considering letting him go because he is so lazy."

"Can I talk to him?"

"Yes, of course. I meant to myself. I'll call him into the house."

"It might be better if we went outside," Kay suggested. "The less Miss Ball and Mr. Minton hear of this, the better."

The two of them bundled up and went out to the barn in search of Stone.

"Ike!" Aunt Jane called impatiently. "Where are you?"

A roughly dressed man with round shoulders and a slightly insolent face came down from the hayloft. Aunt Jane sniffed the air suspiciously.

"You've been smoking again!" she said.

"Well, maybe just a puff or so," the man admitted.

"I've told you time and again I don't want you smoking in the barn! If you disobey my orders again you'll be fired."

"Yes, ma'am."

"What were you doing yesterday?" the woman asked sharply. "Did you fill up the woodbox in the kitchen as I told you to?"

"Sure, I did. While you and the others were out sleigh-riding."

"That must have been when we were at Collston," Kay commented. "Was the house deserted then, Aunt Jane?"

"Yes, except for the servants. Ike, did you go in any of the rooms besides the kitchen?"

"Of course I didn't," the man refuted angrily. "I know my place."

"Well, I guess that will be all," Aunt Jane said, realizing they would get no further with Ike. "Miss Tracey and her friends will want the sleigh this afternoon. Curry the horses and hitch them up right after dinner."

"I was planning to go to town, ma'am."

"You heard my orders! I don't keep a stable for your convenience. Do as you're told."

"Yes, ma'am," Ike muttered, with a resentful expression.

"I dislike that man more each day," Aunt Jane announced, as she and Kay walked back to the house. "As soon as I can find someone suitable to take his place he'll have to go."

"You ought to get rid of him," Kay agreed. "He's insolent and lazy."

Though there was no evidence that Ike had stolen the diamond, Kay could not help suspecting him. She was determined to watch him closely during the next few days.

At one o'clock the sleigh was brought to the door. Ike hitched the team to a post, and then left.

"I guess we'll have to drive it ourselves," Kay said, as she and the twins came outdoors. "Who wants the job?"

"Not me," Betty sang out.

"You'll have to do it, Kay," Wendy added.

Kay didn't mind driving. She had handled the team before and they were quite manageable.

"Where are we going?" Betty asked, as they dashed out of the yard, accompanied by the jingle of sleigh bells.

"I thought we'd make a business trip," Kay smiled. "How would you like to pay a return visit to that village with the movie sets?"

"That'd be fun," Betty instantly agreed. "But why do you want to go there again?"

Kay explained that she hoped to learn more about the Eagle Film Company. The doctor at Collston had given her some interesting information when he had referred to the movie, which had featured a man with six fingers on one hand.

"Surely you don't expect to find that actor still there?" Wendy commented.

"No, but we may be able to find out where he is."

It was a long ride to the village, but the girls didn't mind it. The air was exhilarating, and the sleigh ride was a real treat.

On arriving at their destination, Kay and her friends confirmed that the movie company the doctor mentioned had spent the past summer in the vicinity. They also learned that the watchman in charge of the grounds was not as belligerent as he appeared to be.

"Let's question him," Kay suggested. "The worst he can do is tell us to leave."

They hitched the team to a tree and then returned to the movie lot. They found the watchman in a shack not far from the road. He seemed annoyed at being disturbed but grew more friendly when Kay explained to him that they needed his help. His bad stutter, however, made it difficult for him to carry on a conversation.

"Do you know the present address of the Eagle Film Company?" Kay asked.

"Yes, it's in New York. At s-six, one, one, s-six, one, one, four. Gra-gra——"

"Six, one, one, four?" Kay repeated, writing the number on an envelope.

"No, s-six, o-one, s-six one f-four."

"He never says it the same way twice," Betty whispered to Wendy.

"Here, write it on this envelope," Kay said, offering the man a pencil. "Then I'll be sure to get it right."

Having obtained the address, her next question concerned the actors who had worked on the movie the previous summer. She asked the watchman if he remembered an actor with six fingers on one of his hands.

"S-sure, he was a t-ta—tall, dark fellow," the man stated. "A b-b-bad actor."

"Do you remember his name?"

"His s-s-stage name was S-S-Shad B-Bealing."

"Shad Bealing?" Kay repeated, writing it down on the envelope. "Do you know where he is now?"

The watchman was unable to furnish any further information, except that the movie company had left some of its equipment in storage in a local barn. A few days before a representative of the firm had ordered the material to be shipped by freight to New York. The girls thanked the man for the information and then returned to the sleigh.

"That watchman gave us several valuable clues," Kay commented. "I'm going to write to the Eagle Film

Company and see if they have Shad Bealing's present address."

The trip back to Aunt Jane's took longer than the girls expected. The horses were tired, and Kay didn't want to push them. Twilight was coming on when the sleigh approached a railroad crossing.

"Stop, look, and listen!" Betty ordered. "We don't want to have another narrow escape."

The track was clear in either direction, and the block signals were up. However, several freight cars were standing on an adjoining track. Glancing carelessly in that direction, Kay was startled to see two men stealthily approaching one of the cars.

"Isn't that Ike Stone?" she whispered.

"I think it is!" Wendy agreed, looking closely. "What is he doing here?"

"That's what I'd like to know," Kay said grimly, stopping the team some distance from the tracks so that the jingling sleighbells would not give them away.

The girls tied up the horses and crept quietly toward the siding, keeping themselves well hidden by a dense growth of timber which bordered the road. They saw the two men look carefully around to make certain that their actions were not being observed. Then Ike Stone started tampering with the seal on one of the box-cars.

"Looks like he's about to steal something from that train!" Kay exclaimed. "Let's try to get closer so we can catch him in the act!"

XII

Ike Stone's Shack

The girls crept forward cautiously until they were close enough to the railroad track to hear what the two men were saying.

"This is dangerous business," Stone declared to his companion. "Once we break these metal seals on the car doors, they'll know that someone has been after the stuff inside. The railroad company will have a detective here within a day."

"No one will know who did it," the other man said. "Of course, if you're afraid——"

"Not me. Here goes!"

He broke the seal and opened the door. The two men leaped into the car, looking around with obvious satisfaction.

"This will make a good haul," said Ike. "But we'll have to work fast."

The men had just begun to get to work when there was an unexpected disturbance. The team which the girls had left tied to a tree began to get restless. The horses jerked at their bridles, and one of the animals gave a loud neigh.

The two men in the box-car heard the sound and

darted towards the door. The girls didn't move fast enough and were detected before they had a chance to hide.

Kay moved casually towards the box-car as the two men leaped quickly to the ground.

"Why, Ike, I'm surprised to see you here so far from Aunt Jane's," Kay said innocently.

Ike was clearly uncomfortable. He hastily closed the door but Kay was able to catch a glimpse of the car's interior. She saw several powerful lights like those used on movie sets, an array of sound equipment, and a number of large boxes. It dawned on her that this equipment probably belonged to the Eagle Film Company.

"I live close by," Ike muttered uncomfortably. "I have a cabin in the woods."

"And in your spare time you break into box-cars!" Kay said sharply.

"We weren't breaking in," Ike replied, growing even more confused. "You see, I do a little extra work now and then for the railroad. It helps out on my salary."

"I imagine it would!" Kay retorted. "And your friend, I suppose, is engaged in a similar occupation."

"This is Nathan Blick," Ike said, turning to the other man. Kay noticed that he hesitated before giving the name. "Nathan is a railroad official—an inspector."

"That's right," the man agreed. "An inspector."

As Kay gazed steadily at him, his green eyes shifted uneasily. He wore a cap and tried to keep his face averted so that in the twilight the girls could not get a clear view of his features.

"Just what do you do for the railroad company?" Kay asked.

"Well, I inspect box-cars," the man returned vaguely. "Come on, Ike, we've got to get going."

"Just a minute," Kay said firmly. "I have some more questions for you."

Ike whirled furiously upon her.

"Oh, go on home and mind your own business," he ordered gruffly. "I'm sick of your snooping. You and the old woman are always asking questions!"

The two walked hurriedly away from the tracks and disappeared into the woods.

"Do you really think they were stealing something?" Wendy asked.

"I'm almost sure of it," Kay answered. "I certainly didn't believe that story about their being railroad employees. If we hadn't arrived on the scene when we did, I'm sure they would have stolen some of the film company's equipment."

"Let's look inside the car and find out what they were after," Betty proposed.

Kay shook her head. "No, if we touch the seal we could be accused of breaking it ourselves. After this car is switched onto a freight train the railroad men will discover that the door has been opened. Then the trouble will begin."

"I guess you're right," Betty agreed. "We ought to just go home and report what we've seen."

The girls returned to the sleigh, and in a few minutes were dashing over the hard-packed road towards Aunt Jane's farm. Supper was waiting for them and as they ate they told of their adventure.

"Does Ike Stone work for the railroad company, Aunt Jane?" Kay asked.

"Not to my knowledge. But it's certainly a possibility. Stone is so close-mouthed. He's away about half the time, too."

"We had to unhitch the horses ourselves tonight," said Kay. "Ike was nowhere to be found."

"When he does come back, he'll be fired," Aunt

Jane announced firmly. "I've had quite enough of that man!"

After the meal Kay went to the kitchen to talk to Mrs. Kemp, the housekeeper. The woman knew very little about Stone, though she did confirm the fact that he lived alone in a cabin near the tracks.

"Maybe he does work for the railroad," the woman said. "But he's never mentioned it. I can't imagine him holding down two jobs. He hates anything that entails work!"

"Has he lived in this area long, Mrs. Kemp?"

"No, he came here only a short time ago."

Kay was sure that she and the twins had caught the farmhand in the act of stealing from the railroad car. She believed, too, that he could shed some light on the mysterious disappearance of the diamond ring. However, she was not yet prepared to make a direct accusation.

Meanwhile, Kay was planning a definite course of action in trying to solve the kidnaping case. Her first move was to write a letter to the Eagle Film Company, requesting information regarding Shad Bealing. Among other things she wanted to know if the actor had worn gloves in the picture, and if she might obtain a description of them.

"I'd like to mail this letter tonight," she remarked to her aunt as she stamped it.

"I'm afraid that will be impossible, unless you drive to town. Mail won't be picked up here until nearly noon tomorrow."

"There's a full moon tonight," Betty observed, glancing out of the window. "I wouldn't mind a sleigh-ride to town."

Mrs. Tracey was about to say that she didn't like the idea of the girls going out alone after dark, when Clarence Minton offered to escort them. Miss Ball was asked to accompany the group, but she preferred to spend the evening reading. Minton hitched up the team and drove Kay and the twins to the nearby town of Alton, where they mailed the letter.

"I wish we could look for Ike Stone's cabin," Kay remarked as they started homeward.

"We have time," Minton assured her. "I'm rather curious to see the place myself."

He hitched the team to a tree not far from the railroad tracks, and the girls indicated the path which they had seen the two men take. The box-car containing the movie equipment was still standing on the track.

Following the trail through the woods, the four presently came to a cabin which was half hidden in a dense growth of trees. A dim light gleamed from the windows.

"This must be it," Minton observed. "Should we knock?"

"Not just yet," Kay said.

She crept up to the window and cautiously peered into the cabin. The farmhand and his companion, Nathan Blick, were seated at a table, deep in conversation. Their faces, illuminated by the glow of the lamp, were hard and cruel.

"We'll have to turn the trick tonight," Kay heard Blick say. "Those girls were probably too dumb to realize what we were doing, but the seal on the car has been broken, and if a railroad official should happen along he'd get awfully suspicious."

"You're right," Ike agreed. "Let's finish the job right away. It's dark enough now so we won't be seen."

Kay hastily ducked back from the window and hurried to warn her friends that they must hide. Scarcely had the four retreated behind some bushes, when Ike and Blick emerged from the cabin.

"I just know they're going to rob the box-car," Kay

whispered. "Let's watch them, and then call the police."

When the two men were a safe distance ahead, Kay and her friends followed them cautiously and from the shelter of the woods, watched them slide back the freight car door and disappear inside. After a few minutes the men came out, carrying large boxes on their backs. Staggering under the weight they headed down the trail toward the cabin.

The four observers followed noiselessly, watching while the two men carried the boxes inside the cabin and then emerged for a second load. Once more Minton and the girls hurried after them.

"I'd like to take a look inside that car and see what they're stealing," commented Minton.

He and the Worths climbed inside. Meanwhile, Kay followed the men back to the cabin. So quietly did she slip away, that for a few minutes Minton and the twins did not even realize that she'd gone. Then they, too, returned to the cabin but Kay was nowhere in sight and the cabin was deserted.

"Maybe Kay went back to the sleigh," Wendy suggested.

"Yes, she probably did," Minton agreed. "I'm sure she's waiting for us there though it's strange the way she just slipped away without saying anything."

The three hurried back to the sleigh. Little did they know that at that very moment Kay was in great danger. Kay was determined to find out just what the two men were doing with the film company's property, and in their absence she had quietly let herself into the cabin. As she looked around, there was no sign of any boxes.

"They must be hidden here somewhere," she told herself.

She moved across the floor, and as she did so her shoe struck a hard metal object. It was the ring of a trap-door. Kay lifted it and peered down into a dark cellar. She saw a room filled with numerous boxes, far more than could have been removed from the box-car in one night.

"I have to find out what's in those boxes," she thought.

She darted to the window and looked out. The trail leading down to the tracks seemed deserted. It would probably be several minutes before Blick and Ike returned with another load. Kay decided to take a chance.

Lifting the trap-door again, she quickly went down the stairs into the dark cellar.

XIII

Beneath the Trap-Door

Kay left the trap-door slightly raised so that the light from the lamp would shine down into the cellar. Descending the ladder she wondered if all the boxes piled high in the room contained movie equipment.

She was looking at a strangely shaped box, when she heard the sound of approaching footsteps. A door opened. Ike Stone and Nathan Blick had returned!

Kay had just enough time to squeeze herself flat against the wall between two wooden crates before the two men descended into the basement, carrying several heavy electric motors.

"Say, I told you not to leave the trap-door open," Blick growled. "It's dangerous."

"I did close it," Ike retorted. "Look here! What's this?"

Kay caught her breath as she saw Ike point to a button from her dress lying on the floor.

"Take a look around!" Blick ordered tersely. "It looks like someone's been spying."

Kay was discovered at once. Eluding Stone's grasp, she tried to reach the ladder, but Blick caught her by the arm and pulled her roughly back into the cellar.

"Not so fast, Miss Tracey," he leered. "So you decided to turn detective, did you?"

Kay made no response, thinking that the men would be less harsh with her if she kept quiet. However, her silence merely infuriated them.

"So you won't talk?" Ike cried angrily. "All right, I'll fix you so you can't!"

He pulled a handkerchief from his pocket and used it to gag Kay. Then he tied her hands behind her back, taking pleasure in tying the cloth more tightly than was necessary. Kay clenched her fists together as he fastened the knot, hoping to gain a little slack.

"What should we do with her?" Ike asked. "Leave her here?"

Blick thought a moment, then shook his head. "No, we can't do that. Her friends might come back and look for her. We'll have to get rid of her."

Kay's heart sank as she watched the men drag out a large, empty packing case. Despite her struggling, she was lifted into it. Ike then nailed down the cover, leaving only a small crack for air to come through.

"Maybe they're going to dump me into the lake," Kay thought in terror. "Oh, why did I ever get myself into a fix like this? Mother warned me that I might get in trouble!"

She could hear the two men whispering, but couldn't make out what they were saying. Presently they lifted the crate on their shoulders and carried it down the trail toward the railroad tracks.

From the distance came the shrill blast of a train. The sound sent a chill down Kay's spine. Were those brutes going to put the crate on the tracks of the approaching train?

Ike and Blick had planned a less cruel fate for their victim, however. They set the box down in the snow and waited for the train. Once the train had stopped the two men started looking through the box-cars.

"Here's an empty one," Blick announced, opening the door of one of them. "Shove her in."

Kay felt them lift the crate. She was tumbled over and over roughly as the box was rolled into the car. The two men fastened the door tight and slipped back into the shadow of the trees.

With Kay trapped inside the box, the train began moving.

Meanwhile, Clarence Minton and the twins had returned to the sleigh. They grew very upset when they found that Kay was not there.

"Something must have happened to her," said Wendy anxiously.

At that moment a car drove past, rattling over the railroad tracks.

"That was Ronald Earle!" Betty cried, waving frantically.

Ronald didn't see the little group by the roadside, and his car disappeared around a bend.

"I wonder what he's doing so far from Brantwood?" asked Wendy. "He must have come to see Kay."

"He probably found her and took her back to the house so she could notify the authorities," said Betty. "My guess is Kay then sent him back here to tell us where she was. Unfortunately, he didn't see us."

"I guess she is at the house," Minton acknowledged. "Yet it's strange that she left without telling us."

All three agreed it was time to return to Aunt Jane's. If Kay had not yet gotten to the authorities about the box-car theft, they could do so by phone.

Minton flicked the horses with his whip, and they dashed off briskly, only to be checked by a stiff pull of the reins as they drew near the railroad crossing. A freight train was slowly moving by.

"I wish it would hurry!" Betty complained. "If we want to get the authorities out here before those men get away, we have no time to waste."

The three waited impatiently for the train to pass, not realizing that their good friend Kay was trapped in one of the cars. Finally the caboose clattered by and the road was clear again.

"There's Ronald's car," observed Wendy as the sleigh swung into the familiar lane.

Minton tied the horses up, and Betty and Wendy ran into the house.

"Hello, Ronald," they called out to the tall boy who was warming his hands by the fire.

"Hello! Where's Kay?"

"Didn't you bring her home?" Betty gasped.

"Home from where?"

The twins seated themselves weakly on a sofa. Hurriedly they told Ronald where they had last seen Kay.

"We have to go look for her immediately!" Ronald exclaimed. "I know Kay well enough to be sure that she would go right back to that cabin in the woods. She'd do anything to get to the bottom of a mystery."

"But we looked for her there," Wendy protested. "There was no sign of her."

"Did you look inside?"

"Well, no, Kay wouldn't have gone inside. Those men were going back and forth so often from the cabin to the railroad tracks that going inside would have been too risky."

"Kay wouldn't be afraid to take a little risk," Ronald replied.

"You're right," Betty agreed. "We've got to get back to the cabin as fast as we can. But first we'll have to notify the authorities."

She hurried to the phone and called the sheriff. Then she joined Wendy and Ronald, who were outside talking to Clarence Minton.

"Does Mrs. Tracey know about Kay's disappearance?" the manager asked.

"No," Wendy told him. "Mrs. Kemp just told me that after we left some friends came and insisted upon taking everyone to a little party at a neighbor's house."

"It's just as well Mrs. Tracey doesn't know," Minton said. "After all, it may be nothing at all. I'm sure Kay's all right."

"Of course she is," Wendy agreed firmly, but she was really not so sure. "We'll find her before her mother gets home."

Everyone piled into Ronald's car, and in a short while the party reached the woods which adjoined the tracks. They then set out on the trail leading to the cabin. They were relieved to see a light shining in one of the windows.

"Those two thieves are still there!" Wendy exclaimed. "I hope the police get here in time to catch them."

"So do I," Minton agreed tersely. "But to find Kay will be our first job. I am going to talk to those men and ask them if they have seen her."

"I'll go with you," Ronald offered.

"No, you better stay here with Wendy and Betty. If both of us go it might look suspicious. I won't let on that I know what's been going on here tonight."

"Be careful," Wendy urged anxiously. "Those men are dangerous."

Clarence Minton walked to the cabin and boldly knocked on the door. Instantly the light was extinguished.

"Who is it?" Ike Stone demanded gruffly.

"Clarence Minton. Is that you, Ike?"

The door opened slowly, and Ike looked out eyeing Minton suspiciously.

"What do you want?"

"Kay Tracey has disappeared," Minton stated.

"She hasn't been this way," Ike replied, relaxing slightly as he decided that Minton probably didn't suspect anything. "Maybe she's lost in the woods."

"That's what we're afraid of. You're sure you haven't seen her?"

"Of course I'm sure. If you want to look for her, you can use my lantern."

Ike handed the lantern to Minton and then closed the door in his face. Minton went back to Ronald and the Worth twins, who were anxiously awaiting him.

"Kay's not at the cabin," he reported to Ronald and the twins. "I saw the entire room from the doorway. Ike says he hasn't seen her, either."

"Then she must be lost somewhere in the woods," Wendy said on the verge of tears. "And it's so cold tonight. She'll be frozen before we find her."

"Don't worry," Betty said, trying not to show her own concern. "Kay was dressed warmly. She can't be far away. We'll find her."

"Of course we will," Ronald said firmly.

He ran back to the car to get a flashlight. They separated into two groups, Wendy and Clarence Minton taking the lantern, Ronald and Betty using the flashlight. After mapping out a strip of territory near the cabin, they began a systematic search of it, calling out Kay's name at intervals.

For a long time Betty kept close to Ronald. Thinking that she heard an answer to one of her cries, she dropped back a few paces to listen. Then she saw the guiding light had disappeared.

"Ronald!" Betty cried.

She ran forward quickly to catch up with Ronald. Suddenly she stumbled over a log and plunged head-first into a huge snowdrift.

"Oh! Oh!" she shivered, struggling to her feet.

Then she let out a terrified scream. From the nearby bushes she saw a pair of eyes that glowed like two balls of fire.

XIV

The Girl in the Box-Car

Betty fled in terror. In her haste she forgot about the log and stumbled over it a second time. As she fell face downward into the wet snow, a small animal scurried past, vanishing into the woods.

By this time Ronald had discovered that Betty had disappeared, and had come back to look for her. He started running when he heard her scream, and arrived just as she was picking herself up from the ground.

"Oh, Ronald," Betty wailed, clinging to his arm, "I was attacked by an animal!"

Ronald helped her brush the snow from her clothing and tried to calm her down. Flashing his light over the snow, he revealed small animal tracks leading into the thicket.

"I think your attacker was a fox! It was probably more frightened than you were!" Ronald chuckled.

"A fox!" Betty exclaimed. "I was sure it was a wolf."

"There aren't any wolves in this part of the country, Betty."

Remembering Kay, Ronald's smile faded. Solemnly the two renewed their search, though with a steadily growing fear that they would not find Kay that night.

It had been agreed that after an hour's time the two searching parties should meet at Ike Stone's cabin. When Betty and Ronald returned, weary and discouraged, they found Wendy and Clarence Minton waiting for them.

"Any luck?" Ronald called out.

Minton shook his head. "It's beginning to look pretty serious."

"We'll have to notify the police," Ronald urged.

"The police are here now," said Minton, nodding toward the cabin. "They've promised to help us as soon as they've searched the cabin."

"Have Ike and Nathan Blick been arrested?" Betty asked eagerly.

"No," Minton said with disgust. "Before the police arrived those two crooks skipped off, taking most of the loot with them."

The four went to the cabin to talk to the police. At that very moment Kay was many miles from the scene, imprisoned inside the crate, and being transported to New York.

"If I don't get out of this box I'll suffocate before anyone discovers me," was the frightening thought that flashed through her mind. "I've got to break loose somehow."

Kay struggled and squirmed, but succeeded only in tiring herself. The crate had grown uncomfortably warm, and her limbs were growing numb from her cramped position. At times she felt as if she could not breathe at all.

Kay thought she heard a faint movement of some kind in the car. She tried to work down her gag, but it would not budge.

"If I could get one deep breath of fresh air again!" she thought desperately.

As she shifted her position, her dress caught on a

sharp object. She couldn't see it, but it felt like a piece of metal. With renewed hope she squirmed around until her hands were directly over the rough place on the corner of the crate. Then she sawed the cloth up and down.

She was forced to rest many times, but finally her perseverance was rewarded. The cloth was severed and her hands were free. Kay jerked off her gag, and set herself to the task of getting out of the box. Fortunately Stone and Blick had not nailed the top boards very securely.

Kay located the weakest board, and pried up against it with all her strength but it just wouldn't give. She was about to give up when the nails, with a sudden squeak and groan, suddenly gave way. The board shot upward, and like a jack-in-the-box Kay thrust her head through the opening.

The silence of the box-car was suddenly shattered by a terrified scream. Kay's heart pounded wildly. Someone was in the car with her. Then she made out the dim outline of a figure crouching in a corner.

After a few minutes Kay gathered fresh courage and emerged from the crate. Her movement triggered off another frightened cry from the figure huddled in the darkness.

"Don't be afraid," Kay said quickly. "I won't hurt you."

"Who are you?"

"I am Kay Tracey. And you?"

"Barbara Fountain."

Kay made her way to the opposite end of the car, but it was too dark for her to see the face of the mysterious girl.

"What were you doing inside that box?" the other girl demanded nervously.

Kay related her story. It was bitterly cold in the

car, and the two huddled together to keep warm.

"You're very brave," Barbara said admiringly. "If I were as brave I wouldn't be here now."

"Are you running away from home?"

"I really haven't any home," the girl confessed. "But I am running away from Collston."

"You must have had a good reason for leaving."

"The best ever," Barbara answered, a defiant note in her voice. "If I had stayed in Collston I'd have had to go to jail."

"What did you do?" she asked, "or rather, what were you accused of doing?"

"Oh, I was guilty, all right—that's why I left."

"I hope your crime wasn't very serious."

"I stole some fruit," Barbara said quietly.

Deep in thought, Kay remained silent. Could this be one of the girls Felix Cortez had complained about? She voiced the question.

"Yes," Barbara admitted. "Two other girls helped me. They planned it all out and I just bought the fruit. I guess I shouldn't have listened to them, but I needed food and it seemed like an easy way to make a little money."

"You're about my age, aren't you?" Kay asked.

"Sixteen."

Sensing that Kay was sympathetic, Barbara poured forth her unhappy story. Her mother was dead. Her father was an actor, but he seldom came to Collston to see her because he never seemed to have the time; then, too, he seldom had enough money to make the trip. In recent months he had not even sent her money for food and lodging.

Barbara had been turned out of her rooming house and was in a desperate situation, when two older girls offered to share their quarters with her. They had given her food and clothing. Not until later did Barbara suspect that her roommates had any ulterior motive behind their apparent generosity. Slyly they suggested that she might make some money for herself and at the same time repay them for their trouble, if she would go along with their scheme.

"The way they explained it made the work sound perfectly honest," Barbara said. "I would buy the fruit and have it shipped to a friend of one of the girls who lived in Brantwood. We dealt mostly in crates of oranges, but we also bought other fruits."

"And you then sold the fruit to private parties?" Kay asked.

"The other girls did. But they gave me very little money—only enough to buy food. A week ago the girls said something about the racket playing out and they just left me flat. When they disappeared they owed their room rent. Cortez, the fruit dealer, saw me on the street one day and called the police."

"You weren't arrested?"

"No, I got away. I ran through an alley and made it to the railroad tracks. This freight train was just pulling in. My father is in New York, and I thought that if I could get to him he'd take care of me. I had this basket of fruit and these sandwiches with me, so I just climbed into an empty box-car, and here I am!"

"I guess we're both on our way to New York," Kay sighed. She got up and went to the door. It wouldn't budge when she tried to open it.

"Locked," Barbara announced gloomily. "At Collston it was fastened shut from the outside."

"Then I guess we'll have to stay here until someone comes to unbolt it," Kay said, sitting down again.

She tried to speak cheerfully, but the prospect of being stuck in the cold box-car for hours or even days was not pleasant. Barbara's story had deeply moved her. While she did not approve of the girl's actions she did feel very sorry for her.

"Maybe I can help her when we reach New York," she thought. Then it occurred to her that without money she would be in need of help herself.

The train rattled and bumped along until the steady rumble of the wheels finally lulled Kay to sleep. When she woke up several hours later she was very hungry.

"Have some of my sandwiches and fruit," Barbara said. "It was lucky that I had this basket of food with me. When my landlady kicked me out of the rooming house I took what little food was left with me."

Kay gratefully accepted something, but both girls ate sparingly, realizing that if they were trapped in the box-car for several days they would need to make the food last.

They soon lost all track of time, sleeping as much as they could, and at intervals talking and eating. Although the train made frequent stops no one opened the car door.

Kay was aroused from one of her naps by the sound of someone at the door. She quickly nudged Barbara and the girls scrambled to their feet. Suddenly light flooded the interior of the car. A burly man peered in at the two girls.

"A couple o' lady tramps, eh?" the trainman said. Then, as Kay and Barbara tried to escape through the door, he said, "Oh, no, you don't!"

"Let us go!" Kay cried. "Our being in this car is a big mistake."

"It was a mistake, all right," the trainman agreed with grim satisfaction. "I'll have to turn you over to the police."

"Oh, please let us go!" Barbara pleaded.

"I have orders to arrest anyone caught stealing rides."

"But it was all a mistake," Kay insisted. She told him how she had been imprisoned in the crate and showed him the broken crate to prove her words.

"Sounds like nonsense to me," the man said doubtfully. "But I'll call an official and see what he thinks."

However, the girls had no intention of staying around that long. The instant the man turned his back, Kay motioned to Barbara to follow her, and they leaped down from the car. As a hand truck loaded with boxes and crates was wheeled along the platform, they jumped aboard.

"This is what I call riding in style," Kay chuckled, crouching with Barbara behind a large wardrobe trunk.

Her high spirits didn't last long, however. The trainman, realizing that the girls had escaped, caught a glimpse of Barbara's red beret sticking up above the luggage.

"Hey, you!" he shouted furiously, running after them. "Get down from there!"

XV

A Chase

Kay and Barbara leaped from the truck and darted down the tracks.

"Stop them!" the trainman shouted.

Two yard guards chased after them. The girls, with a good start, dodged this way and that between trains, finally reaching the street, breathless but happy.

"Well, here we are in New York," Kay declared wearily. "We look like tramps. And we're hungry and penniless."

"I'm not broke," Barbara stated. "I have two dollars."

"Two dollars! Why, you're rich!"

"It won't do me much good, but you'll at least have enough to phone your friends. You can pay me back later if you like."

"I certainly will," Kay promised. "And with interest!"

The girls stopped at the first drug store along the busy street, grateful just to be inside a warm place. They noticed the clerk eyeing them suspiciously, but he said nothing when Kay went into a phone booth. She put some change in the slot, and asked the operator to reverse the charges on a call to Aunt Jane's. After what seemed like a long wait she was connected. Mrs. Tracey was overjoyed that her daughter was safe, but upset to hear that she was so far away.

"Oh, I'm so glad you're all right!" she exclaimed. "You have no idea how worried we've all been. Searching parties are scouring the countryside for you."

After reporting her adventure Kay talked to Bill, who assured her he'd send her money immediately. Finally she talked to Miss Ball, who insisted that she and Barbara stay in her apartment while in New York.

"I'll let my maid Jeanne know you're coming," she promised. "After such a harrowing trip you need a confortable place to rest."

Kay thanked her and carefully took down the address of the apartment.

Kay saw Barbara standing near the lunch counter, gazing hungrily at a bowl of hot soup which a clerk had ladled out to a customer.

"Let's have something to eat," Kay urged. "We have enough money."

Kay ordered two bowls of soup, careful to leave herself enough money for cab fare to Miss Ball's apartment. Kay and Barbara couldn't help but laugh as they saw their reflections in the mirror above the soda fountain. Their clothes were wrinkled and covered with bits of straw and lint; their faces were drawn and pale. At this point, however, all that was really on their minds was the hot soup they so desperately wanted.

Kay found a kind taxi driver, who agreed not to turn on his meter but simply charge the girls whatever they could afford.

"Now we're completely penniless," said Kay in the cab. "But we're riding in more style now than we were an hour ago!"

The girls were relieved to finally reach Miss Ball's apartment. They rang the bell and a petite French girl in white apron and cap admitted them.

"Kay Tracey?" she inquired, pronouncing the name with a slight accent. "And Barbara Fountain? I was expecting you. Miss Ball phoned a few minutes ago. My name is Jeanne."

She led the girls into an elegant room furnished in a modern style. While Kay and Barbara were taking off their coats, the maid went to draw water for their baths.

"This is a fantastic apartment," Barbara said when the two girls were alone. "It was certainly nice of Miss Ball to let us stay here."

After the girls had taken their baths the maid insisted that they both lie down and rest. While they ate breakfast served on silver trays, Jeanne searched her mistress's wardrobe for clothes that would fit the girls.

"I never thought a boiled egg could taste so good," Kay sighed blissfully.

"Would you like another," Jeanne asked.

Kay shook her head. "I've had enough, thank you."

She leaned back against the pillows and turned her head to gaze at Barbara. During the long ride in the box-car she had tried to imagine how the girl looked, but her appearance did not seem to match her voice. Barbara was very thin, with deep shadows beneath her eyes. Although her mouth was too large for the rest of her face, she did have a nice face and on those rare occasions when she smiled, some might have called her pretty.

After a while Kay dropped off to sleep. But she was soon awakened by the ringing of the phone. As she grew dimly aware of her surroundings, she heard Jeanne Prix's excited voice.

"No, Monsieur Purcell, Miss Ball is not here. No, Monsieur, I cannot tell you when she will return. You will call again? *Très bien.*"

A moment later the maid came into the bedroom looking worried and disturbed.

"That man—he has been calling for the past three days! I do not know if I should give him Miss Ball's address and phone number. She did not leave instructions."

"Did I hear you say the man's name is Purcell?" Kay asked.

"*Oui*, he is an old friend of Miss Ball. But I think she does not wish to see him again."

"You were right not to give him any information," said Kay. "This is not a friendship Miss Ball would want to revive."

"He will call again," Jeanne frowned. "I do not know how to discourage him."

Kay and Barbara dressed themselves smartly in the clothes which the maid provided, and spent the greater part of the day reading and listening to records. Several times Barbara mentioned that she wanted to locate her father.

"I'll help you tomorrow," Kay promised. "By that time my money will be here."

Late that afternoon Kay received the money Bill had sent. She tried to give Barbara some cash but she refused to accept it.

"I won't need any money after I find my father. He'll take care of me. Oh, I can hardly wait to see him again!"

As she looked at the girl's happy face, Kay hoped that nothing would get in the way of a reunion. Early the next morning the two girls set out for the boarding house that was the most recent address Barbara had for her father. It turned out to be in a squalid section of the city. When Kay asked the landlady if Mr. Fountain lived there, the woman glared at the two girls somewhat insolently.

"No, he doesn't live here any more, I'm glad to say!"

He was unpleasant and slow with his rent. I was glad when he packed up and left!"

"Do you know where he lives now?" Kay asked.

"No, I don't. He didn't leave a forwardin' address."

Before Kay could ask any more questions, the woman closed the door. Barbara was so disappointed she burst into tears.

"Don't cry," Kay comforted her. "We'll find your father."

As the girls were walking away, the door of the boarding house opened and a short, bald man came running after them.

"Were you two asking about Fountain?" he called. "I could not help but overhear."

"Yes, we were," Barbara replied quickly. "Do you know anything about him?"

"I roomed next door to him for three months. A few days ago he got into a hot argument with someone—a tall, thin fellow who came to his room. They had a fight and Fountain was beaten up."

"Oh!" Barbara exclaimed in horror. "Was he seriously hurt?"

"No, but he was in bed for a couple of days. When he was able to get up he packed his luggage and skipped out."

"Do you know where he went?" Kay asked.

The man shook his head. "He didn't leave any address. I don't think he wanted anyone to know where he was going."

This information completely discouraged Barbara. During the ride back to the apartment she said scarcely a word.

"I'll start looking for a job tomorrow," she said, when the two girls had returned to the apartment. "I can't stay here."

"We may be able to find your father yet," Kay encouraged. "Don't give up hope."

She was thinking over the problem of Barbara's future, when the electric buzzer rang. It was a signal that a visitor had entered the downstairs lobby.

"I'll answer it," Kay called to Jeanne, who was busy in the kitchen.

She went to the house phone and asked, "Who is it, please?"

"Harry Purcell," came the indistinct reply. "May I come up?"

Kay hesitated. She was sure Beatrice Ball would not have wanted this man admitted to the apartment, yet she wanted very much to talk to him for a few minutes. She felt he might be able to throw some light on the kidnaping.

"Come on up," she told him.

In a few moments she met the man in the corridor. He was a middle-aged man whose face was marred by a black and blue spot under his right eye.

"Mr. Purcell?" Kay asked.

"Yes."

"I'm Kay Tracey. You don't know me, but I have heard Miss Ball speak of you."

"We were formerly associates," the man stated proudly. "Is she here now?"

"No, that's what I wanted to talk about. A few days ago an attempt was made to kidnap her."

Kay had expected her news to startle the man, but the expression on his face did not alter. His reaction led Kay to think that he knew something about the matter.

"Perhaps you read about it in the papers," she questioned.

"Yes, I believe I did."

Kay knew that Purcell had not learned of the attempted kidnaping through the press, because Bill had managed to keep Miss Ball's name out of the papers. When she pointed this out to Purcell he did not appear disturbed.

"Well, I don't mind admitting, Miss Tracey, that I learned of the kidnaping from another source."

"Then perhaps you can tell me who was responsible."

"Perhaps I can," he agreed, smiling significantly. "Yes, if you make it worth my while, I might be able to give you an interesting clue!"

XVI

A Reunion

"Tell me how I can make it worth your while," Kay urged.

"I am very low in funds right now," Purcell said with a smirk.

"You mean you want money. Is that it?"

"Yes, Miss Tracey."

Kay found it hard to conceal her dislike for the man. She'd heard nothing good about him and she was beginning to understand why.

"I came here to see Miss Ball," the man said hurriedly, observing that Kay was displeased. "I'm sure she'll be happy to give me the money."

"As an old friend of hers, I'd have thought you'd be glad to help her—without being paid for the service."

"I need the money," the actor returned lamely. "She has plenty of it."

"I don't believe you have anything worth selling. It's no mystery who was responsible for the crime. The kidnaper left a clue behind, so it's only a matter of time until he's caught."

Purcell was clearly disappointed. Kay suspected that he did in fact have information about the case, and was not attempting to get money under false pretenses.

At that moment the door to Miss Ball's apartment opened and Barbara emerged. When she saw Purcell, she stopped short, then uttered a happy cry.

"Father!" She flung herself into the arms of the surprised man.

As the two began to talk excitedly, Kay urged them into the apartment and closed the door. She was utterly bewildered by the scene she had just witnessed. The man who called himself Purcell was none other than the missing Mr. Fountain. But why did he call himself Harry Purcell? Kay asked the man to explain himself.

"Fountain is my real name," he said somewhat sheepishly. "Miss Ball always knew me as Purcell, as that is my stage name."

"And Barbara is your daughter?"

"Yes. I'm afraid I haven't looked after her the way I should have," he said sadly.

"I came to New York to see you," Barbara said eagerly. "At the rooming house they told me you had moved away."

"Oh, yes—yes. I moved to a nicer place."

"I'm glad to hear that, because I didn't like the place very much. I was afraid you might be having trouble again—money trouble."

Fountain's face flushed, and he avoided Barbara's eyes.

"Do you have work now?" she asked.

"Well, not at the moment," he admitted reluctantly. "But I'll find something soon."

Kay sensed that Barbara wanted to be alone with her father, so she tactfully excused herself and went into a bedroom. She was afraid that the reunion was not destined to be a happy one. Barbara had begun to suspect that something was wrong; on the other hand, it was obvious that Mr. Fountain was worrying that he would not be able to support his daughter.

"I'd like to help her," Kay thought. "But I certainly don't feel like paying her father for information."

From the living room the voices grew louder and louder. Kay decided to leave the apartment.

Now would be an excellent time for her to visit the offices of the Eagle Film Company. She found the number in the phone book and called to make an appointment.

"This is Miss Kay Tracey," she explained. "I'm a friend of Beatrice Ball's."

Mention of the actress's name confused the secretary. She thought that Kay was none other than the famous actress herself. However, Kay was not aware of the confusion.

"We'd be delighted to see you today," the young woman purred. "Mr. Toner will expect you at three o'clock."

Kay thought she'd wear the dress she had worn on the train. However, Jeanne told her it had not yet been returned from the cleaner's.

"We'll pick out another of Miss Ball's outfits for you. She won't mind. She instructed me to provide you with everything you might need."

Together they selected something and while Kay dressed, Jeanne phoned for the chauffeur.

The door to the bedroom opened, and Barbara came in.

"Has your father gone?" Kay asked quickly.

"Yes, he just left."

Kay could tell that Barbara was upset but felt that this was not the time to question her.

Just then Jeanne announced that the car had arrived. Kay said good-bye to Barbara and left the apartment. The chauffeur politely doffed his cap as he swung open the car door.

It was a short trip to the Eagle Film Company.

When Kay reached Mr. Toner's office, she spoke to the secretary with whom she had made her appointment.

"My name is Kay Tracey. I have a three o'clock appointment."

"You're not Beatrice Ball! I'd never have given you an appointment if you hadn't resorted to a trick!" the secretary said furiously. "Leave this office at once!"

XVII

A Deserted Apartment

Kay tried to explain the misunderstanding, but the angry secretary wouldn't listen. In the midst of it all the door to Mr. Toner's office opened, and a bald-headed, heavy gentleman of middle age, stepped out.

"What's going on out here?" he asked sternly.

"This girl got an appointment with you by saying she was Beatrice Ball," the secretary said tartly.

"That's not true," Kay denied. "I did not say that I was Miss Ball. I can explain the mistake."

"Tell your story," the president said unexpectedly.

Kay gave an account of the events which had led up to her present predicament. She was pleased to see the tense expression on Mr. Toner's face gradually relax.

"Well, well, I don't see that any harm has been done," he said genially. "Why do you wish to see me, Miss Tracey?"

"I can't very well tell you here," Kay said, glancing at the secretary, who was still looking at her with distrust. "However, it concerns a kidnaping."

"Oh, now I remember!" the president exclaimed. "You wrote me about it, didn't you?"

"Yes, several days ago."

"Come in," the man said cordially, standing aside for her to pass. "Your letter interested me very much."

He offered Kay a chair and carefully closed the door.

"If I remember correctly, Miss Tracey, you mentioned a six-fingered glove in your letter."

"Yes. It was worn by the man who attempted to kidnap Miss Ball."

"You requested information concerning one of our actors—I have forgotten the man's name."

"Shad Bealing."

"Oh, yes. What is it you want to know about him?"

"I'd like to get his present address. I'm also eager to find out if he has an extra finger on his right hand."

"Am I to assume that you suspect one of our actors of attempted kidnaping?"

"I'm not drawing any conclusions just yet. I'm only trying to get information."

"I'll do anything I can to be of assistance," Mr. Toner promised.

He pressed a buzzer. When his secretary answered he asked her to have a Mr. Elberton come to his office. While waiting for him, Kay asked the president about the movie that had been made near Collston.

"It has not yet been released nor titled," he explained. "One of the characters in the story was a man with six fingers, but that's all I can remember about it. Mr. Elberton, who was the director, should be able to tell you more."

Elberton was short and very nervous. He willingly answered all of Kay's questions.

"Did Shad Bealing work on a recent movie for you?" she asked.

"Yes he did."

"Do you have his present address?"

"I may be able to get it for you, though I doubt it. Bealing was just an extra."

"Do you remember anything about him?" Kay asked hopefully.

"Sure, he was a strange fellow—morose and bad tempered. He had an extra finger on one hand."

"The right or the left?"

"I believe it was the right."

"So far the description fits the man I'm looking for," Kay declared with satisfaction. "If I could only see him I might be able to solve this case."

"We could show you the movie in which he appears," the director offered. "Would that help?"

"It might. Thank you very much."

Mr. Elberton escorted her to a nearby room, where he made arrangements for a screening of certain portions of the movie. The first glimpse of Shad Bealing's face made Kay grip her chair. She recognized him instantly as the person she had seen driving the tan car near the street corner where Betty had been hit. And probably he was also the kidnaper of Miss Ball!

The actor looked even more sinister on the screen than he had in real life, for his face had been made up to inspire horror.

The picture itself, though shown in unrelated sections, interested Kay. It was the story of a beautiful actress who had been kidnaped. Kay wondered if Shad Bealing might not have been inspired by the story to kidnap Miss Ball and hold her for a large ransom.

The lights flashed on, and Mr. Elberton turned to ask Kay if she had recognized the actor.

"Yes, and I'm sure he's the kidnaper. If you can give me his address I'll be most grateful."

"I'll see what I can do," the director promised. "Wait here."

He was gone nearly half an hour. Kay had begun to think that he had forgotten her entirely, when finally he returned.

"Sorry to have kept you waiting," he apologized. "And now I must disappoint you, too."

"You couldn't find the address?"

"No, it was never recorded. Bealing had only a small part in the picture. We used him because of his deformity, not for any acting ability."

Kay was extremely disappointed to find herself at this dead end. However, she was deeply grateful to Mr. Toner and Mr. Elberton for their assistance and before leaving the offices thanked them both for their kind cooperation. They in turn promised that if Shad Bealing could be traced, they would let her know immediately.

As Kay rode back to Miss Ball's apartment, she concluded that on the whole the day had been a successful one. Personally she was confident that Shad Bealing had been responsible for the kidnaping; yet she realized that the authorities would need more substantial evidence before arresting the man. They would say that Kay could have been mistaken in her identification of him.

She had seen the driver of the tan car from a distance, and the occasion had been a dark, stormy night when visibility was poor. Then, too, she did not have proof that the man who had kidnaped Miss Ball was the same person who had hit Betty, although the clues certainly pointed to this conclusion.

"If I could only locate Bealing, Miss Ball should be able to identify him definitely," Kay thought.

Kay didn't know how to go about tracing Shad Bealing. She doubted that the Eagle Film Company would be able to help her further. As soon as she had left the office, she thought of many questions she wished she had asked the men. It also occurred to her that she hadn't mentioned anything about the theft of movie equipment from the box-car near Collston.

"I'd like to find out if Ike Stone and Nathan Blick were stealing material from the Eagle Film Company," she reflected. "If I don't have the opportunity to talk again to the president, I'll write him a letter and tell him what I know."

Her thoughts went back to Shad Bealing. She felt she must try to locate him.

"There's one clue I haven't investigated," she told herself. "Barbara's father hinted that he knew the identity of the kidnaper. Maybe he can tell me where to find Shad Bealing."

When she arrived at Miss Ball's apartment building Kay hurried up in the elevator and rang the door bell, but no one came to the door. She was somewhat worried because both Jeanne and Barbara were at home when she had left the place only a short while before.

"Either the buzzer is broken or something has happened," she thought.

She tried the door, and found to her surprise that it was unlocked. As she entered, a cloud of dense smoke poured into the hall.

"Jeanne! Barbara!" she called loudly.

Her cries went unanswered. The whole apartment was in disorder. The furniture was not in its usual place, and as she made her way toward the kitchen she stumbled against an overturned chair.

"Jeanne! Jeanne!" Kay shouted.

She thought she heard a muffled groan, but could not tell where it came from, so she pushed on. Smoke was rolling out of the kitchen in great black waves. The odor was overpowering. The girl's eyes became blinded.

"Jeanne and Barbara are probably trapped behind the flames," she thought desperately. "I must reach them before it is too late!"

XVIII

A Rude Visitor

Groping her way toward the entrance to the kitchen, Kay saw that the apartment was not in flames as she had feared. Instead, Jeanne had left the dinner cooking on the stove and it had burned to a crisp. Smoke was pouring out of several red hot kettles.

Coughing and choking, the girl fought her way to a window and opened it. Then she darted to the stove and snatched the blackened pots from the fire. Observing smoke seeping from the oven, she opened it and was nearly overcome by a great inky cloud which poured into the room. Recovering herself, she drew out a pan of charred biscuits and tossed them into the sink.

"Oh! This is awful!" Kay exclaimed. "Whatever could have happened?"

She ran from one room to another, opening windows. The apartment appeared to be deserted.

As Kay approached a storage closet she heard a muffled groan. Quickly she jerked open the door. The maid, gagged, with her hands tied behind her back, crumpled to the floor at Kay's feet.

"Jeanne!" Kay cried in dismay.

She untied the gag, and cut the rope which had been used to bind the maid's hands together. Jeanne was unable to talk until Kay had given her a glass of cold water.

"Tell me what happened!" she cried.

"I was preparing dinner in the kitchen when a strange man came in——"

Suddenly they heard an excited murmur of voices in the hall. Jeanne's story was interrupted by the arrival of several neighbors. They had seen smoke pouring into the corridor and thought the building was on fire. While Kay was explaining the situation to them, other residents joined the excited little group.

When the commotion was at its height they heard a fire engine clanging down the street. Kay ran to the window and looked out to see the fire engine stop in front of their building.

"Did someone call the fire department?" she asked.

"Yes, I did," a man answered. "When I saw all that smoke I thought your place was on fire."

"Hurry down and tell the firemen that we don't need them, please," Kay urged. "If they shower us with water after all we've been through, it will be a calamity!"

Gradually the air in the apartment cleared, and the last visitor was escorted to the door.

"Now tell me what happened," Kay said to Jeanne.

"I was getting dinner," the maid related, "when a strange man rang our buzzer. I couldn't understand what he said, so I let him come upstairs. He wanted to speak to Miss Ball and I told him she wasn't in."

"Did he give his name?"

"No, I asked him what it was and he said, 'None of your business.' I tried to close the door but he blocked it with his foot. Before I could prevent him, he came right into the apartment."

"It wasn't Purcell?" Kay questioned. "Barbara's father?"

"Oh, no, I would have recognized him at once; in fact, he was here only a few minutes before this stranger appeared."

"I didn't mean to interrupt your story, Jeanne. Please go on."

"I tried to scream, but the stranger clapped a hand over my mouth. He bound me and locked me into the closet."

"Then I suppose he searched the apartment."

"Yes, I heard him moving about near the desk. Oh, dear, I don't know what Miss Ball will say when she hears of it. Do you think she will fire me?"

"I am sure she won't," said Kay. "It wasn't your fault. Can you describe the man who locked you in the closet?"

"I was too scared really to look at him, Miss Tracey. He had a dark complexion, I think, though I can't say for sure."

"By the way, where's Barbara?"

"Why, she left right after you went to the movie office."

"Where did she go?"

"I don't know, but she said she was leaving for good. She left a note for you."

Jeanne went to the desk where she had left the note, but everything was in disorder. At first Kay was afraid that the message might be lost, but after straightening out the various papers Jeanne found it.

The note explained very little. Barbara had written only three short sentences which sounded impersonal and slightly disconnected.

"I am going away with my father. If you see Miss Ball I wish you would express my appreciation to her for the use of her lovely apartment. And thank you for your own kindness to me."

Kay did not speak for a moment. She was sorry Barbara had left. She remembered that when they had parted only a few hours before, the girl had seemed strangely quiet.

"Barbara must have known then that she was going to leave," Kay thought. "She was afraid to tell me for fear I might try to prevent her."

After reading the message a second time she folded it and put it in her purse.

"When did Barbara leave?" she asked Jeanne.

"Very soon after you did. Her father came for her and they went away together."

"Did she say where they were going?"

"No, Mademoiselle. I noticed that she was crying when they went out the door."

Kay sighed. She hoped that Barbara would be happy with her father, but the tears were a bad sign. Purcell had chosen to vanish at a most awkward time. Now it would be difficult for Kay to learn if the information he had tried to sell her concerned Shad Bealing.

As she stood looking out the window, she saw a taxi drive up to the door. A man and a young woman got out. Kay looked at them disinterestedly, then suddenly realized who they were.

"Jeanne!" she called. "Miss Ball and Mr. Minton are here!"

The maid ran over to the window. Recognizing her mistress, she flew about the apartment in a futile attempt to restore it to some semblance of order.

"Never mind," Kay said kindly. "I'll explain everything."

She met the actress and her escort at the door and was joyfully greeted by the pair. When she entered the apartment, the young woman gazed about her critically and sniffed the air.

"Burnt food! And the place is all torn up! Jeanne, what's happened?"

"We've had a lot of excitement here the past hour," Kay answered.

"Didn't you have enough of that on your wild ride to New York?" Minton inquired with a chuckle.

"Apparently not. But this excitement wasn't of my own making. I suspect that if Miss Ball had been here the adventure would have taken on a more serious aspect."

She then recounted all that had happened. To this the maid added some details of her own, enlarging upon the incidents to impress her mistress.

"That stranger may have been the man who tried to kidnap you!" Minton exclaimed, turning to Miss Ball.

"That's very likely," Kay agreed. "And I firmly believe Shad Bealing is the one we should go after."

She mentioned the evidence she had gathered that afternoon at the offices of the Eagle Film Company.

"You certainly haven't wasted your time since you reached New York," Minton commented admiringly. "So you think Bealing is the kidnaper?"

"Yes, I do. He seems to fit the description perfectly. The problem is, how do we find him?"

Minton asked Jeanne for a description of the mysterious stranger, but the maid was unable to provide it; nor could she say if the man had an extra finger on his right hand. She had been too terrified to notice anything.

While Miss Ball was going through her desk to see if anything of value had been taken, Minton gave Kay news of her family.

"Your mother has been terribly worried about you. She was in a state of near collapse until you phoned.

Then she was afraid you'd have trouble alone in New York. She was greatly relieved when Miss Ball and I decided to cut our visit short and return to the city. That ride in the box-car must have been terribly frightening. You might have smothered to death in that crate. Jail is far too good a place for Ike Stone and Nathan Blick."

"Haven't they been captured yet?"

"No, but the police are hot on their trail. Your cousin is personally helping them."

Their conversation was interrupted by the electric buzzer. Jeanne answered the call and came to report that a Mr. Elberton was below.

"Why, he was the director with whom I talked this afternoon!" Kay exclaimed. "Did he ask to see me?"

"No. Miss Ball."

"Oh!" A puzzled look came over Kay's face, then she smiled. "I guess he's here to check up on my story."

In fact, that was the reason why the man had come. Kay's story was quickly confirmed and then Kay took the opportunity to mention that she had witnessed the theft of the movie equipment. "Did it belong to your company?" she asked.

"Yes, it did," the director answered. "We've been trying to find out who stole the material."

Kay gave him the names of the two thieves and gave a description of each of them.

"I hope they'll be caught," she said. "I have a personal reason for wanting to see them put in jail."

"Don't worry, that's where they'll be very soon," Elberton promised. "We'll have private detectives on the case in the morning."

"If you do arrest Ike Stone I'd like to speak to him," Kay said.

"Consider the request granted," the director smiled as he picked up his hat. "Ike is the same as captured now."

After Mr. Elberton had departed Minton prepared to leave, saying that he intended to stop by the Eagle Film Company offices. With his hand on the doorknob he turned and looked quizzically at the Tracey girl.

"I suppose when you give Ike the third degree you'll be able to get square with him for his meanness to you."

Kay looked startled. "He deserves harsh treatment but I'd prefer someone else give it to him. My sole object in wanting to question Ike is to find out what he did with Shad Bealing's diamond ring!"

XIX

A Package of Money

"Then you think Ike Stone was the one who stole the diamond?" Miss Ball inquired.

"I'm positive of it," Kay affirmed. "Isn't it logical that if he would steal from the film company he wouldn't hesitate to steal from Aunt Jane's house?"

"Yes," the actress agreed slowly.

"It's one thing to believe Ike's guilty and another to prove it," Minton observed.

"Of course," Kay admitted. "We'll have to find some way to make him admit the truth. It won't be easy, though."

"You'll have to catch him first," the manager said dryly.

The three friends discussed the situation for a few minutes longer, then Minton left. Kay and Miss Ball helped Jeanne straighten up. Then Jeanne was sent to the store for groceries. During her absence, Miss Ball brought up the topic of Shad Bealing.

"I didn't want Clarence to know this," she confessed nervously, "but I haven't had a peaceful moment since that man tried to kidnap me. I'm afraid he'll try it again."

"Bealing is a dangerous character," Kay agreed. "I feel sure he's the one who broke in here."

"Obviously he was expecting to find me. I'm so afraid he'll return."

"That is possible," Kay admitted. "I wonder what he's after. Probably money."

"I'd be willing to pay him a large sum if I were sure he would never bother me again," Miss Ball declared earnestly. "The suspense of not knowing when he's going to strike next is making a nervous wreck of me."

"We all hope Bealing will be caught soon," Kay comforted. "Now that we know his identity, it should be fairly easy to trace him."

"He's awfully cunning. I'm afraid the police won't catch up with him. In that case I'll never have another comfortable moment. If I thought I could get rid of him by paying him some money I'd gladly do it."

Kay disapproved of anything of the kind, and moreover she felt that the scoundrel would probably pocket the money and later make further demands.

Clarence Minton returned to the apartment at dinner time, reporting that his meeting with the president of the Eagle Film Company had been highly satisfactory. Mr. Toner had promised that no expense would be spared in tracking down the two men who had robbed the box-car.

Shortly after dinner Minton went to his hotel, which was several blocks away. Miss Ball and Kay were ready to retire when the phone rang.

"Will you answer it for me?" the actress asked wearily.

Kay lifted the phone from its hook.

"Is this Miss Ball?" a guttural voice demanded.

The girl hesitated a fraction of a second before answering, for she sensed that something fishy was going on.

"Can I take a message?" she requested.

"No," the voice retorted shortly. "I must speak to Miss Ball and no one else."

Kay put her hand over the mouthpiece and called to her friend.

"I have a funny feeling that it's Shad Bealing," she whispered.

"Let me talk to him," Miss Ball said excitedly.

"Don't let him frighten you," Kay warned.

Miss Ball's eyes widened with fear as she learned the identity of the caller. It was indeed Shad Bealing, the mysterious owner of the six-fingered glove.

"Yes, I'll do as you say," Kay heard the actress promise rashly. "If you'll agree never to bother me again, I'll give you the money. Yes, tomorrow night at nine o'clock, wherever you say. I promise not to call the police. You can trust me to keep my agreement."

Miss Ball hung up the receiver. As she did so, she turned to face Kay, who regarded her somewhat reproachfully.

"I know I shouldn't have done it," the actress acknowledged. "But my peace of mind will be worth the price."

"How much did you agree to give him?" Kay asked.

"Five thousand dollars."

"And where is the money to be delivered?"

"I am to wrap it in a package and take it to Central Park tomorrow night at nine o'clock."

"You're not planning to take it there yourself!" Kay exclaimed.

"I must. Bealing said that I alone should bring it there."

"Mr. Minton will never let you, I'm sure of it," Kay said.

"Oh, he won't know about it until later," Miss Ball

declared hastily. "You must not tell anyone, Kay. Promise!"

"All right," the girl agreed unwillingly. "However, I think you're making a mistake not to call in the police. They could lie in wait and capture Bealing when he appears at the park."

"No, I have given my word and I must not break it. It's too risky. You'll help me, won't you, Kay?"

"Yes, I'll do anything I can."

"I'll have you go to the bank for me first thing in the morning. I told Clarence I wouldn't leave the apartment without letting him know. He is so worried about me."

"How are you to meet Bealing without breaking your promise to Mr. Minton?" Kay asked.

"I hadn't thought of that," Miss Ball admitted.

"I have an idea! I will take your place."

"You'll deliver the money to Bealing?"

"Yes. Why not?" Kay demanded eagerly. "Everyone says I look a little like you. It will be dark and if I dress in your clothes I'm sure I can get away with it."

"I wouldn't want you to take the risk."

"It won't be as risky for me as for you," Kay insisted.

"I don't know what to say," Miss Ball answered slowly. "I'll think it over during the night."

But by morning she had not yet reached a decision. As soon as the bank was open Kay carried a special order signed by Miss Ball, receiving in return a neat package containing five thousand dollars in denominations of twenty-dollar bills.

Before returning to the apartment with the money Kay made another stop along the street, but was careful to make no mention of this to Miss Ball.

"You will let me deliver the package, won't you?" she urged Miss Ball as the day wore on.

"All right," the actress consented. "I'll have my chauffeur drive you there. I feel confident he would guard you with his life, should the need arise."

"Maybe it would be better not to tell him that I am taking your place?"

Miss Ball agreed it was worth a try.

Although Jeanne prepared an excellent dinner, both Kay and Miss Ball ate very little. They watched the clock nervously as the moments sped by.

"I ought to start dressing," Kay announced when the gong struck seven. "I want plenty of time to get ready."

Miss Ball and Jeanne assisted her. When they had finished, Kay was highly pleased with the result. She was sure she could pass for Miss Ball.

The first test came when she greeted the chauffeur, who had been ordered to bring the car to the entrance.

"To Central Park, please," Kay directed, imitating the actress's voice as best she could.

"Yes, Miss Ball," the driver said politely.

They reached the appointed place at ten minutes before nine, but Kay had planned to arrive early. With the package of money carefully hidden under her coat, she walked rapidly toward a clump of trees which Bealing had designated as the meeting place.

"I only hope my plans turn out right," she thought uneasily. "Perhaps I should have told Miss Ball what I intend to do, but she might not have agreed, so I guess it's best that I didn't."

Kay glanced alertly in all directions but could see no one.

"I hope Bealing appears," she told herself. "If he doesn't it will ruin everything."

At ten minutes after the hour, Kay began to lose hope. She was chilled to the bone from the cold, biting wind. Suddenly she heard a step behind her. She whirled about to face a uniformed messenger boy.

"You are Miss Ball?"

Kay murmured something the boy accepted for yes.

"I will take the package," he told her. "Return to your car and do not follow me. You understand the instructions?"

"Yes," Kay acknowledged.

She held out the parcel. The boy took it and disappeared in the darkness, as Kay walked swiftly to the waiting car. Suspecting that she was being watched, she got in the car, but immediately stepped out on the opposite side. Simultaneously a taxi drew up and she entered it. Miss Ball's chauffeur, according to instructions given him previously, promptly drove away.

"Everything worked out exactly right," Kay chuckled to herself. To the driver she said tersely, "Follow that uniformed messenger boy and don't let him get away. He took the left hand road leading out of the park."

"I'll keep him in sight, Miss," the man promised.

Kay leaned forward in her seat, anxiously watching for the boy who had disappeared with the money. If she could only trail him, she felt sure that he would lead her directly to Shad Bealing. A moment later she was greatly relieved to glimpse the boy getting into a car which had been parked on the main highway ready for a quick getaway.

"There he is!" she directed her driver. "Keep far enough back so that he won't suspect he's being followed."

The driver nodded, and applied himself to the task of keeping the mysterious car in sight. It wound in and out of side streets, coming presently to a railroad station. Kay got out, asking the driver to wait for her, and followed the messenger into the building.

She saw him walk directly to the north side of the waiting room and hand the package of money to a tall, thin man. As Kay had anticipated, he turned out to be Shad Bealing. The blackmailer gave the boy a coin, and hurriedly made his way to a window, where he bought a ticket. Then he stepped out onto the platform to board a train.

The instant he had disappeared, Kay darted to the ticket office. She learned from the agent that Bealing was enroute to a town named Shelbourne.

"Why, that's not far from Aunt Jane's!" Kay thought excitedly.

The train had gone and there would not be another until morning.

"I must reach Shelbourne before he does," Kay reasoned. "The only way to do it is by plane!"

The waiting taxi carried her to an airport. Thanks to Bill's generosity, she had plenty of money and was able to charter a plane that could take off in ten minutes.

"I must phone Bill and Miss Ball," Kay thought.

It took so long for the operator to connect her with her cousin, that she did not attempt to explain the real reason for her unexpected trip. Anyway, someone might overhear her. Instead she said tersely:

"I have decided to come home by plane tonight, Bill. I'm leaving soon. Will you meet me at the Shelbourne railroad station? Be sure to come—it's extremely important!"

Scarcely waiting to hear Bill's assurance that he would be waiting for her, she hung up and then got Miss Ball on the wire.

"Oh, I'm so glad you're all right," the actress declared. "I was beginning to worry. Did you deliver the package?"

"Yes," Kay answered, "but I have only a minute to talk to you. I'm leaving by plane for Shelbourne. I'm going to try and head off that man."

"Don't try it," Miss Ball pleaded. "I can afford to lose the money, but if anything should happen to you I'd never forgive myself."

"I'll be in no danger," Kay reassured her. "Before I go I must tell you about the money. It is safe."

"Safe?" the actress echoed blankly. "But I thought you gave the package to Bealing."

"I did, but I played a little trick on him. I substituted a package of fake money, leaving only an outer covering of genuine bills."

"You clever girl!" Miss Ball gasped. "Where is the rest of the money?"

"You'll find it hidden in your apartment. Look in the big Chinese vase."

While Miss Ball was thanking Kay profusely for what she had done for her, an attendant came to the door to tell the girl that her plane was ready. She said a quick good-bye to Miss Ball.

Kay wrapped her coat more tightly about her as she stepped into the cabin of the plane. The trip to Shelbourne would be a cold one.

"All set?" the pilot grinned.

"All set," Kay repeated, smiling.

The plane roared down the runway, nosing into the biting wind. It took off smoothly, and was soon lost in the enveloping night.

XX

The Twins' Discovery

When Bill Tracey turned from the phone after talking to Kay, he was besieged with questions from Mrs. Tracey and the Worth twins.

"I don't know what it's all about myself," he protested. "Kay is coming to Shelbourne by plane and she wants me to meet her at the railroad station."

"But why not at the airport?" Mrs. Tracey inquired. "Are you sure you didn't misunderstand her?"

"No, she said the railroad station. She was excited and didn't have time to explain very much. But I suspect she's on the trail of that man who lost the six-fingered glove, or else she has a clue about Nathan Blick and Ike——"

He broke off suddenly, realizing that one of the maids, Lucy Cupp, was standing in the doorway listening intently to the conversation.

"You'll not be needed here, Lucy," Aunt Jane said sternly.

"Yes, ma'am," the girl murmured, hastily retreating to the kitchen.

"That girl is a good worker, but she isn't overly bright," said Aunt Jane.

"Have you noticed that whenever Ike Stone's

name is mentioned Lucy always seems to be around?" Betty remarked when the maid was out of hearing.

"I wonder if she isn't a bit interested in Ike Stone?" Wendy asked thoughtfully.

Mrs. Tracey and Aunt Jane did not hear the remark, for they were talking to Bill about the trip to Shelbourne. However, Betty drew her sister into the hall.

"I think you struck the nail on the head that time, Wendy. I've suspected for two days that Lucy was infatuated with Ike. Whenever his name is mentioned she blushes and acts very silly."

"Maybe she knows where he is, Betty."

"That's exactly the thought I had! Before Kay gets back let's do a little detective work of our own."

"She'll be here in a few hours. We'll have to be quick."

"Then let's get to work on Lucy right now!" Betty proposed.

The twins found the maid sulking in the kitchen. She felt that she had been severely spoken to by Aunt Jane. At first Lucy would not talk, but gradually Betty and Wendy put her into a better frame of mind. They discovered that the girl had a deep admiration for Kay. This explained in part why she always listened to everything that was said about her.

The twins introduced the farmhand's name casually into the conversation. When they did so, Lucy smiled rather sheepishly, and blushed.

"Ike is a fine man," she declared. "He has more class than the other farmers around here. He's more like a city fellow."

"It's strange he left so suddenly, isn't it?" Betty stated.

"Oh, I know where he went," Lucy announced importantly.

"To New York?" Wendy prompted.

"California. Ike doesn't like the climate here—he finds it very unpleasant."

"And very likely it will get more so," Betty commented under her breath. Lucy did not catch the real meaning, however, for she had no suspicion that the twins were deliberately leading her on to reveal more information about Ike Stone.

"I suppose you hated to see him go," Wendy remarked.

"Yes, I did," Lucy confessed. "But before he left, Ike gave me something to remember him by."

"A piece of jewelry?" Betty prompted alertly.

"Yes, a ring. I'll show it to you if you won't tell anyone he gave it to me."

Betty and Wendy exchanged looks, but were careful to make no such promise as Lucy requested. Overlooking their silence, the girl removed a diamond ring from a black velvet ribbon around her neck.

"Isn't it pretty?" she asked proudly. "I'd wear it on my finger, only Ike told me I shouldn't until he gets back from California. I imagine we'll be married then."

Betty and Wendy stared at the ring in amazement. They immediately recognized it as the diamond Kay had found tucked away in the six-fingered glove. Obviously Ike had stolen the ring from Kay's bedroom.

"Isn't it pretty?" Lucy repeated impatiently as the girls remained silent.

"Oh, yes, yes indeed," Betty answered hastily. "It must be very valuable."

"I think Ike's been saving up a long time to buy it. I wish he hadn't made me promise not to wear it."

Wendy was on the verge of blurting out the truth about the ring, when Betty, guessing what her sister was about to say, shot a warning glance at her. At that moment the housekeeper entered the kitchen and nothing more was said about the matter. When they were alone again the twins had an animated discussion.

"It won't do any good to tell Lucy the truth," Betty argued. "Let's wait until Kay arrives."

"Maybe that would be the best thing to do," Wendy agreed.

The girls were determined to accompany Bill Tracey when he drove to Shelbourne to meet Kay. They found him in the garage, and asked if they could go with him.

"It will be a long, cold ride," Bill pointed out. "We may get stuck in a snowdrift on the way."

"We'll help you dig out the car," Betty laughed.

"I'll remember that. If you're awake when it's time to leave, you can come along."

"We'll be awake, all right," Wendy announced.

The plane was scheduled to reach Shelbourne at a very early hour in the morning. Bill Tracey and the twins planned to leave the house shortly before midnight. The girls were ready at the appointed time, but when they went to the garage they found Kay's cousin working over the engine of the car.

"The darn thing won't start," he complained. "Run back into the house where it's warm. I'll soon have it going."

An hour later he was still laboring in the garage. Betty and Wendy, watching from the kitchen window, grew more and more uneasy.

"We'll never reach Shelbourne on time now," Wendy said.

Finally, when they had given up all hope of carrying out their plans, they saw a puff of black smoke spurt out from the open garage doors.

"Come on!" Betty shouted, catching her sister by the hand. "He has the car started."

Bill coaxed the motor carefully, feeding it gasoline

gradually until it was running smoothly. The twins closed the garage doors and leaped into the seat beside him.

"How late are we?" Bill asked anxiously as they drove down the lane to the main road.

"Nearly an hour," Betty told him. "If Kay's plane is on time we'll never make it."

"I don't know what made the car act up that way," Bill said irritably. "I'll drive as fast as I dare, but the roads are slippery."

Although Kay's flight was an uneventful one, headwinds were strong and the trip took longer than she had figured on. She nervously consulted her watch every few minutes. When at length the plane descended upon the Shelbourne airfield, it was over half an hour behind schedule.

"Bill will be waiting for me at the railroad station," Kay thought. "I must hurry. And it doesn't leave me such a lot of time to get ready for Bealing."

The pilot insisted on accompanying her in a taxi to the railroad station. When they reached it, Kay was disappointed that Bill was not there.

"Something must have delayed him," she sighed.

"Perhaps he's been and gone," the pilot suggested.

Kay asked the agent on duty if anyone had asked for her, but the man assured her no one had.

"When does the sleeper from New York arrive?" she inquired.

"It's on time, so it'll be here in an hour. Expecting someone?" he asked. "Or do you want a ticket?"

"I'm—going to meet a passenger," Kay replied. "My cousin, Bill Tracey, will be arriving soon. If he asks for me will you tell him I'll be back in half an hour."

"All right, Miss," the agent promised.

Kay held a whispered conversation with the pilot, and together they left the station. They had asked the cab driver to wait, and now directed him to go to the police station.

"I had no idea you are a young detective," the pilot remarked as they drove along. "If I had, I might have been nervous in the plane," he laughed. "But I'm glad you told me about this affair, and I'll help you out until your cousin arrives."

"Thank you," said Kay. "I'll be perfectly safe as soon as I reach the police station."

At headquarters Kay explained the situation. The chief told her that two men would be sent to meet the incoming New York train.

"If that blackmailer is aboard we'll arrest him," the chief promised.

Kay asked if she could go back to the station with them, and they agreed. At that point the pilot said good-bye, wishing the girl good luck.

"We'll leave here in fifteen minutes," said the captain to Kay. "Make yourself comfortable in the meantime."

On the way to the station, Kay gave the policemen a complete description of Bealing. When they arrived she was disappointed again to find that Bill had not yet arrived. However, she had only a few minutes to worry about him, for presently she could discern a tiny light far down the track.

"Oh, I hope everything will work out all right," she thought excitedly as the beams grew larger.

Presently the train came puffing into the station, its cars covered with snow and icicles. Passengers began unboarding. The officers eyed each person critically.

Kay's eye swept across the long row of windows, nearly all of which were covered with frost. In the front part of one of the cars she saw a man reading a newspaper, his hat pulled low over his eyes. At first glance she thought it was Bealing, but she was not certain.

Kay did not guess that the blackmailer had been quick to observe the policemen. He immediately suspected that they were waiting for him, and accordingly had shoved his baggage far under the seat and moved away from the window.

"It looks as if your man isn't on this train," one of the detectives remarked to Kay.

"I'm sure he is," she maintained. "I think I caught a glimpse of him."

"We'll search the coach," one of the men said.

The two policemen swung aboard the train just as it began to pull slowly out of the station.

"I hope they'll be able to recognize Bealing," Kay murmured to herself.

She eyed the moving cars, half tempted to follow the officers aboard. However, at that moment her attention was distracted by the roar of an automobile which had driven up to the railroad platform. Instantly she saw Bill and the twins.

She cast a regretful glance after the departing train and hastened to greet her friends.

XXI

An Unfortunate Escape

Shad Bealing, seated aboard the train, saw the two policemen enter the coach directly ahead of him. Nervous about this turn of events, he took his light handbag, which contained the package of fake money, and slipped into the vestibule.

By this time the train had picked up speed. Bealing opened the door of his coach and looked out. The thought of jumping paralyzed his muscles, and he could not move.

He stood on the lowest step, his bag in his hand, watching the telephone poles whiz by. Presently the train slowed down for a bridge. Bealing decided to seize this opportunity to make his escape.

Shortly before the train reached the bridge, he jumped. He struck the ground harder than he had expected to, and rolled over and over. He lay in a ditch where he had fallen, moaning in pain.

Just then two men came walking along the tracks. Bealing raised himself on his arm and hailed them. They reluctantly acknowledged his cries.

"What's the matter?" one of them asked.

"Can't you see?" Bealing snapped. "I fell off the train! Don't stand there staring! Help me up!"

"Looks to me as if you jumped off," the other man commented as he helped Bealing get up.

"Well, even if I did, it's none of your business! Pick up my bag over there by the bushes. No, give it to me! I'll carry it myself."

The two men, who chanced to be Nathan Blick and Ike Stone, were suspicious of Bealing, but his hostile demeanor warned them not to be inquisitive. They noticed that he kept his face averted deliberately and that he had a black glove on his left hand.

"I suppose we'll have to take him to the cabin," Blick commented in an undertone to his companion.

They half carried the injured Bealing along the tracks until they came to a trail which led at right angles through the woods. Although he was in pain, Bealing would not permit either Stone or Blick to carry his bag.

The cabin was pleasantly warm. As the three men entered, a young girl was just putting on her coat and hat to leave.

"Are you going, Lucy?" Ike inquired.

The girl stared at Bealing before answering. During the absence of Bill Tracey and the Worth twins from the farmhouse she had slipped away to prepare some food for the two men. Although Lucy had led Betty and Wendy to believe that Ike had left for California, she had known all the while that he was staying in a cabin in the woods. She did not, however, realize that she was assisting a criminal, for the box-car theft had never been discussed in her presence.

"Yes, I'll have to get back," the girl responded, her eyes still fastened upon the injured man. "While you were away I baked some beans and a couple of pies."

"You're terrific," Ike praised.

"Say, that food smells good," Bealing commented gruffly.

"Are you hungry?" Lucy inquired timidly.

"Half starved. I was too busy today to do much eating."

"I'll get you a plate of beans," Lucy offered. "And I'll wrap up your arm, too, if you'll let me."

"Go ahead," Bealing growled.

Lucy heated water and washed Bealing's arm. She improvised a bandage which she wrapped over the wound. Bealing eyed the girl intently as she worked. This made her so nervous that she spilled half a kettle of water on the floor. She noticed that he kept his right hand in his pocket.

"I'll have to be going now," Lucy repeated when she had finished her task.

"Here, wait," Bealing commanded unexpectedly. "Bring over my bag from the table."

Lucy obeyed. Bealing opened it and took out a small roll of bills. He peeled off two of them.

"Here is something for you," he offered.

Lucy reached out to take the money. As her fingers closed over the bills, Bealing suddenly snatched them from her. With a low exclamation of rage he examined the money under the lamplight. Then he flung it angrily to the floor.

"Cheated! Tricked!" he shouted furiously. "If I had that young woman here now I'd break every bone in her body!"

Terrified at such an outburst, Lucy fled from the cabin. She ran through the woods and did not slow down until she reached the main road.

As she nervously waited for a bus, Bill Tracey and his party drove by, enroute to Aunt Jane's.

"Maybe we ought to give that poor girl a ride," Wendy said sympathetically. "It's so cold and the bus may be late."

"Why, it's Lucy Cupp!" Kay cried. "Do stop, Bill."

Bill stopped on the side of the road. The girls hailed the maid, who eagerly accepted an offer of a lift.

"You're out pretty late tonight, aren't you, Lucy?" Bill inquired dryly.

"I went to visit a friend," the girl answered. "I had such a terrible experience! I ran all the way to the road!"

"What happened?" Kay asked.

"While I was cooking some food for Ike and his friend they came to the cabin with a strange man."

"Why, Lucy," Wendy interrupted severely, "just this evening you told us that Ike had gone to California."

"I meant to say he's going there in a day or two," the maid corrected, in confusion. "Oh, dear, I wasn't to tell that, either."

"And you say this stranger frightened you?" Kay questioned quickly.

"Yes, he had been injured in jumping off a train. His arm was hurt and I wrapped it up for him. Then he offered me two bills. I started to take them but he snatched them away, yelling something about being cheated and tricked. He acted so wildly, I ran off."

Lucy was astonished when the twins burst into laughter.

"I don't see anything funny about it," the maid protested.

Kay instantly grew thoughtful.

"She must have encountered Bealing!" she decided excitedly. "He was furious because he discovered that I had substituted fake money for the ransom cash."

By this time they had reached the farmhouse. Lucy was sent off to bed, whereupon Kay and her friends held a conference. Kay told of her suspicions regarding the stranger at the cabin.

"Do you think she told the truth about those three

men being in the cabin together?" Bill asked. "She's so scatter-brained. I wonder if we can trust her."

"Lucy's story sounded straight enough to me," Kay returned. "Shad Bealing must have panicked when he saw the two policemen board the train at Shelbourne. He probably jumped off and was injured."

"I'd like to have seen his face when he discovered that you tricked him!" Betty chuckled.

"Of course, it may all be a trumped up story," Bill reasoned. "If Lucy told one lie she could easily tell another."

"Her only lie was that Ike had gone to California," Wendy answered. "He must have warned her not to reveal his hideout."

"Lucy has Bealing's ring," Betty informed Kay. "Ike gave it to her, but I don't think she knows it was stolen."

"I always thought that Ike took it," Kay said. "We must notify the police and have them surround the cabin. What a grand *coup* it would be if we could capture all three scoundrels at one time!"

Quickly Bill went to phone the authorities. During his absence, Wendy remembered that a letter had come that afternoon for Kay. She gave it to her at once.

"Aren't you going to read it?" Betty asked, as Kay thrust the envelope, unopened, into her pocket.

"Perhaps I should," Kay admitted. "I really was thinking of something else."

Absently she ripped open the flap and glanced at the message which had been written on cheap writing paper. Then she uttered a little cry of surprised delight.

"It's from Barbara Fountain!"

XXII

News from Barbara

"Who is Barbara Fountain?" asked Betty.

"She's the girl I met in the box-car. While we were staying at Miss Ball's apartment she ran off without saying where she was going."

Eagerly Kay read the long letter.

"What does she say?" Wendy inquired curiously.

"This letter explains a number of things that have puzzled me. And it definitely establishes Shad Bealing's guilt!"

"But what is the connection between him and Barbara?" Betty asked.

Kay handed the note over to the twins. Its contents were amazing. Barbara had written that her father, known to Miss Ball as Purcell, had confessed to a part in the kidnaping.

"That's incredible!" Betty exclaimed. "That possibility didn't occur to anyone, did it?"

"I suspected that Fountain knew who the kidnaper was," Kay said, "but I never once dreamed that he was involved. I guess that explains why Barbara was afraid to stay at Miss Ball's apartment."

Barbara had written that Purcell, angry at the way Miss Ball had treated him years before when they were partners, had suggested to his friend, Shad Bealing, that they attempt to extort money from her. Bealing immediately became interested in the idea and made plans to kidnap the actress.

Purcell, in the meantime, began to lose courage. If the plot failed, both he and Bealing would probably have to face long prison terms. He tried to persuade his crony to abandon the idea. Bealing apparently agreed, but a few days later he decided to attempt the kidnaping alone.

"When Miss Ball eluded him, Bealing thought that Purcell had warned her of the plot," Kay explained. "Later he went to Purcell's room and severely beat him."

"Then Barbara's father really wasn't guilty of the crime," Wendy commented.

"Not of the kidnaping," Kay agreed, "but he made a big mistake by trying to get Miss Ball to pay him for information regarding Bealing."

"Barbara doesn't try to excuse her father," Wendy observed, reading the final paragraphs of the letter. "She says here that they both realize they've made serious mistakes, but they hope to get a fresh start in a new community."

"She has a job, too," Betty added, glancing over her sister's shoulder.

"Notice that she doesn't say where it is, nor does she give her new address," Kay said quietly. "Perhaps it is just as well. If we were to keep in touch with each other she'd only be reminded of her unhappy past."

After Wendy and Betty had finished reading the letter, Kay put it back in the torn envelope and locked it away in Aunt Jane's desk. The letter would serve as evidence against Bealing, though Kay would not use it unless she was forced to. She didn't want to implicate Barbara's father in the crime.

Bill came back after his phone call and reported that the police were on their way to the cabin in the woods.

"I had a hard time convincing them that it wasn't another false alarm," he declared. "The cabin has been searched again and again, but Stone and Blick have always managed to elude the officers. This time I think they'll be caught."

"I wish we could drive back there," Kay said.

"There's really little we can do, now that the police have been notified," said Bill.

"I suppose you're right," Kay acknowledged. It had been a strenuous day, and Kay was very tired. It was plain to her now that the net was gradually drawing around Shad Bealing. She could not help but want to witness his capture.

"Let's all go to bed and get some rest," Bill said wearily. "In the morning we can drive to the police station and present our evidence."

Kay and the twins trudged upstairs to their rooms, leaving Bill to turn out the lights and lock the door.

Kay did not prepare for bed immediately; instead, she sat by the window and watched the moon rise over the pine trees. She was thinking of Barbara Fountain, and hoped that wherever the girl had chosen to make her new home, she would be happy.

Presently her attention was drawn toward the trees which bordered the lane. She could see the shadowy figure of a man approaching the house. He was carrying a lantern. Some distance away he halted. Then he raised and lowered the light three times in swift succession.

"A signal!" Kay thought.

She tiptoed to the bedroom door and listened. Directly above her she could hear the sound of footsteps. Someone was leaving the servants' quarters by the back stairs.

"I bet it's Lucy Cupp!" she told herself. "She's probably going out to meet Ike Stone!"

Quickly waking up Betty and Wendy, Kay went back to the window to watch. Her suspicions were soon confirmed. She saw Lucy quietly let herself out of the house and hurry down the lane to meet the man with the lantern.

"We must follow!" Kay told her friends. "Hurry and dress."

Leaving the house, the girls caught a glimpse of Lucy and Ike far ahead, walking toward the main road.

"It looks like the police didn't get to the cabin in time to make an arrest," Kay remarked in disappointment. "Otherwise he wouldn't be here now."

"I wonder why he wants to see Lucy at this time of the night?" Betty speculated.

"Perhaps he's working on a new plot," Kay said. "I wish we could listen to their conversation."

The couple ahead had stopped near a clump of bushes, and were speaking in low tones. Kay and the twins did not dare get any closer lest they be seen. They were too far away to hear what was being said, although now and then they caught a few words.

The girls were so intent upon watching the couple that they didn't notice a car parked in a clump of trees along the road. They didn't realize that Bealing and Blick, now fast friends, had accompanied Stone to the farmhouse and were waiting for him. However, the two men, hidden by the shadow of the trees, were watching the girls intently.

It was clear that something Lucy had said had angered Ike. The girls heard him speak harshly to her, whereupon she burst into tears. Ike then turned his back on her and walked away swiftly. Lucy stood staring after him, crying as if her heart would break.

"Poor thing!" Wendy said sympathetically. "Let's try to comfort her."

She and Betty ran over to the maid and tried to console her. Kay was about to join them when she heard a slight movement in the bushes behind her. She turned around but not quickly enough.

Shad Bealing and Nathan Blick sprang from out of the shadows. Before Kay could scream, one of them clapped a hand roughly over her mouth. Then they dragged her back from the road and out of sight among the trees.

XXIII

Fire!

Kay struggled to free herself, but in the strong grasp of the two men she was helpless; nor could she cry out to Betty and Wendy who were only a few yards away.

Bealing and Blick forced Kay into the car where Ike Stone sat waiting. Before the twins were even aware that Kay was missing, she was being driven off toward a cabin in the woods, not the one where they had kept the stolen movie equipment.

When they arrived at the cabin Bealing carefully locked the door. Then he removed the handkerchief which covered Kay's mouth.

"Why have you brought me here, Shad Bealing?" Kay asked, eyeing him defiantly.

"So you know my name?" he sneered. "Yes, Kay Tracey, you are entirely too smart. I'll teach you to play tricks on me!"

With his uninjured hand he caught Kay roughly by the shoulder. As she whirled away from him, she cried, "Your glove! Why do you wear only one?"

The question distracted Bealing for a minute. Involuntarily he jerked his right hand behind his back.

"I lost the other one somewhere," he muttered.

"Is this it?" Kay demanded, producing the six-fingered glove which was in the pocket of the coat she had grabbed up before leaving the house.

Bealing snatched it from her.

"Yes, that's it." Then, instantly realizing his admission might be damaging to him, he said, "At least, it looks a little like mine."

As he spoke, Bealing examined the fingers of the glove.

"You won't find the diamond ring if that's what you're looking for," Kay said. "It was removed long ago."

"You stole my ring!" Bealing exclaimed.

"So you admit it was yours?" Kay smiled. "No, I didn't steal it. It just so happens that Miss Ball inadvertently snatched this glove from the hand of the man who attempted to kidnap her."

"It's a lie!" Bealing snarled. "I've never heard of an actress by that name."

"I don't recall mentioning that she was an actress," Kay smiled.

Bealing flushed angrily and moved toward the girl menacingly.

"What have you done with the ring? Give it up or I'll——"

He left the threat unsaid, but Kay sensed from the expression on his face that he was not in a mood for arguing. She had pushed far enough.

"Ask Ike Stone what happened to your ring!" she retorted.

"Don't try to hang this thing on me!" the farmhand shouted. "I don't know anything about any ring!"

His voice had a frightened, insincere note which Bealing was quick to detect. He eyed Ike suspiciously.

"What about that big diamond you gave Lucy and asked her not to wear?" Kay reminded him.

"If she told you I gave her a ring, then she lied!"

"My friends saw it," Kay retorted. "It was the very same one I found in Bealing's glove. You stole it from my room at Aunt Jane's."

Ike started to deny it, but Bealing cut him short.

"You double-crosser! You pretended to be my pal, and all the while you had my ring!"

As Kay had anticipated, the three men argued violently. At the height of the commotion she slipped noiselessly toward the door. Bealing saw her, however, and blocked her path.

"Get some rope!" he commanded sharply. "We'll tie this young woman up until we've settled our differences."

Kay was bound hand and foot. Ike Stone seemed to take a cruel delight in drawing the cords as tightly as possible.

"This time you won't get away," he sneered. "You were clever to escape from the box-car. I'd like to see you loosen *these* ropes!"

He drew them so firmly that she winced with pain. Ike laughed.

"See here," Blick said when Ike had finished the task, "why quarrel any more about that diamond ring? This girl probably said what she did just to cause trouble among us."

"Of course she did," Ike agreed. "I don't know anything about the ring."

Bealing, however, chose to believe Kay over the two thieves. He made a cutting reference to the box-car robbery, which in a foolish moment Ike had told him about.

"If you stole from the railroad company, you probably took the ring, too!"

"Don't you throw that in my face!" Stone hissed. "You're no saint yourself! A blackmailer and a kidnaper!"

With a snarl of rage Bealing sprang upon Stone. Blick joined in the fight to help his friend. The chairs were overturned and one of the windows was broken. Bealing, it was certain, was being severely beaten.

Suddenly Kay thought she heard an indistinct sound outside the door. She listened intently, hoping that the police had arrived. Turning her eyes toward the window, she was startled to see Bill peering into the cabin. Her heart leaped. He had brought help!

Kay assumed that Bill had brought help. However, Bill was not only alone but he was unarmed. When Wendy and Betty realized that Kay was missing, they lost no time in calling Bill. He had noticed signs of a struggle in the snow and had traced Kay and her kidnapers to the road where their car had been parked. While the twins had been alerting the rest of the family, Bill had driven off to pick up the trail.

The sight of Kay tied up incensed Bill. He flung open the door and burst in on the struggling men. He fought his way to his cousin's side, but before he could untie her Bealing had sprung on him. Then the two rolled over and over on the floor.

Kay tugged frantically at her ropes but succeeded only in drawing them tighter about herself. She could not be of any help to Bill. Bill was an unusually strong, athletic man, but no match for three opponents.

"Look out!" Kay screamed, as Ike Stone raised a bottle over Bill's head.

Bill dodged it, and dealt the farmhand a stunning blow which sent him reeling against the wall.

By this time the interior of the cabin was a complete wreck. All but one window had been broken, and the outside door was half battered down. A gust of snow blew against Kay's cheek, but she was too terrified to notice or even care that the weather had suddenly assumed the proportions of a blizzard.

Though Bill put up quite a fight, he was finally overpowered by the three men and given a severe beating, the sight of which brought tears to Kay's eyes.

She pleaded with the men to stop, but it was only when they became weary that they finally stopped.

Ike tied Bill's hands behind his back and fastened him securely to a wooden chair. Although blood streamed from a face wound he eyed Ike unflinchingly.

"Next time you'll think twice before you meddle," the man sneered.

"You win this trick," Bill said grimly, "but the deal isn't finished. Within forty-eight hours you'll all be behind bars!"

Ike laughed contemptuously.

"Come on," Bealing urged nervously. "We've got to move out of here! You waste too much time talking, Ike."

The three men quickly pulled together a few of their possessions. In his haste to get out, Blick accidentally brushed against a lantern on the table which miraculously had remained intact during the fight. He attempted to save it but failed. It crashed to the floor, oil spilling in every direction.

"Now you've done it!" Bealing cried.

In an instant the floor was ablaze. The flames spread rapidly, fed by the brisk wind which came in through the open doorway.

"Come on!" Ike shouted. "Let's get out of here!"

Abandoning Bill and Kay, the three men fled from the cabin.

XXIV

A Desperate Situation

Kay and Bill watched the circle of flames as it crept closer and closer. They struggled frantically but were unable to free themselves.

"Let's scream for help!" Kay cried. "Maybe someone will hear us!"

They shouted together, repeating their call over and over. The wind flung the sound back at them as if in cruel mockery.

"It's no use," Bill gasped. "We're doomed."

With horror they watched the leaping red tongues come closer and closer. Fanned by the breeze, the fire was spreading rapidly. It wouldn't be long now before the whole cabin would be ablaze.

Kay prayed that Betty and Wendy would bring help but deep down she knew that escape would have to be the result of their own efforts.

Bill tugged at his ropes until his wrists were raw and bleeding. Weakened by the beating he had taken, his endurance suddenly gave way. His head slumped down on his chest, and he seemed to lapse into unconsciousness.

"Bill! Bill!" Kay cried, almost hysterically.

Bill seemed to be out cold.

In sheer desperation Kay tipped over the chair to which she had been tied, deliberately throwing herself toward the creeping line of flame. Rolling over, she held her hands above the fire, letting the flames lick against the ropes. She endured the pain, knowing that this was her only hope of freeing herself.

Kay's sleeve caught fire, but at the same instant the rope severed and she was free. Quickly beating out the flames, she darted to her cousin's side. The knots of his bond had been tied so tightly that she could not unfasten them. Gasping for breath, she found a knife in a drawer of the table and cut the ropes.

She shook Bill vigorously until he opened his eyes. Half dazed, he leaned heavily on her shoulder as she led him to the door. They staggered outside, drawing the fresh air deeply into their lungs.

Moments later a wall of the cabin fell.

"Another minute, and we would have been burned to death!" Kay exclaimed.

Bill, whose face was white as death, made no response.

"How do you feel?" Kay asked with alarm.

"I'll be all right," Bill replied weakly. "I'm just a little battered up from the fight."

They stood for a moment watching the blaze. The wind had died down considerably and the snow, which was falling steadily, tended to keep the flames under control so that there appeared to be no danger of the nearby trees catching fire.

"Let's get out of here," Kay urged, taking Bill's arm to steady him.

"I parked the car not far from the road."

"Do you think you'll be able to make it?"

"Yes, I feel better than I look, Kay. I'll make it."

Having to make a path through the drifts as they

went it took them some time to reach the place where Bill's car had been parked.

"Why, it's gone!" he cried. "And so is Ike Stone's car which was parked near mine."

"The men must have taken both cars," Kay groaned. "Now what are we going to do?"

The snow was falling so rapidly now that within a short while every trail leading from the woods would be obliterated. Bill scarcely had strength enough to fight his way through the deep drifts, yet Kay hesitated to leave him behind while she went for help. The attorney sensed the thought which was passing through her mind.

"We've got to get to the main road," Bill said grimly. "I can make it."

"Lean on me," Kay pleaded.

"No, you go ahead and clear a path."

In some places the drifts came almost to Kay's waist. She trudged through them, making as wide a path as she could. Although her progress was slow, Bill lagged behind. It was obvious that his strength was failing rapidly.

Kay paused and looked back. "Watch out for a boulder—" she warned, but her words were spoken too late.

Bill tripped over the rock and fell face downward in the snow. Kay ran back and helped him to get up, but the man's feet crumpled under him.

"You're completely exhausted," Kay observed in alarm. "We'll rest a while."

They sat down on a log, huddling together for warmth. Bill's head wound had begun to bleed again, and Kay sopped the blood with a handkerchief. Soon they were both covered with a thin blanket of snow. Kay's feet and hands began to grow numb.

"It can't be far to the road," she said anxiously. "Do you think you can make it now?"

"I think so."

With Kay's help he staggered a few feet, and then collapsed.

"It's no use, Kay. I can't make it."

"We'll rest again."

Bill shook his head, stifling a groan as he did so. "You go for help," he urged. "I'll wait here."

Kay didn't want to leave him alone, but she felt she had no choice. Even if he rested a while longer she doubted that he would be able to continue any farther. It was bitterly cold, and if they stopped moving they could freeze to death.

"Go on, Kay," urged Bill. "You can bring help in about half the time it would take me to get to the road."

"I'll hurry as fast as I can. Stay in the shelter of this tree until I return."

Kay hugged her cousin and then trudged away through the snow. She was chilled to the bone and very weak, but she just had to get to the main road. She kept thinking of Bill and wishing that she had not left him, yet she knew that she could not have done otherwise.

Just as she was beginning to think that she was lost, Kay caught a glimpse of the road ahead. When she reached it she broke into a run. Her heart leaped as she saw a farmhouse beyond the first bend.

Kay pounded on the door until a light came on on the second floor. The farmer and his wife quickly came downstairs and let her in. While Kay quickly explained Bill's predicament the man hitched up his sleigh.

The farmer worked swiftly, but Kay was desperately afraid that Bill might freeze to death before help could reach him.

At last they were off. The sleigh was well

equipped with heavy blankets and heated bricks which the farmer's wife had supplied.

"Which way?" the farmer asked.

"To the left," Kay directed.

The horse was a spirited one and gave his driver considerable trouble.

"Maud was trained for the race track," the farmer explained. "Sometimes she's a bit frisky and hard to handle."

"I think we're coming to the turn-off," Kay said, watching the roadside intently. "Yes, I am sure this is it."

The man pulled on the left rein, but scarcely had the sleigh entered the woods than Kay began to doubt that she had given the right directions.

"Now which way?" the farmer asked.

"To the right, I think," Kay said doubtfully. "Oh, dear, this doesn't look familiar, either."

As they progressed deeper into the woods, Kay began to worry that she had made a mistake. The farmer stopped the sleigh, surveying his surroundings.

"See here, Miss, this can't be right. We passed this spot five minutes ago."

"We've traveled in a circle!" Kay gasped in panic. "Oh, I'm all mixed up. I don't know where to look now."

The farmer had relaxed his grip on the reins, allowing them to rest loosely in his hand.

At that moment, a small animal darted across the path and the horse bolted.

The sleigh tilted sharply sideways. Caught completely off guard, Kay and the farmer were hurled into a huge snowdrift.

XXV

Captured

Kay emerged from the drift and shook the wet snow from her clothing. A short distance away the farmer was getting to his feet.

"That horse!" he muttered.

Maud and the sleigh had disappeared into the woods.

Suddenly Kay started to laugh. The farmer stared at her in amazement.

"Maud threw us out at exactly the right spot!" she chuckled. "Now I know where I am."

She ran through the woods, calling Bill's name. Following his answering cry Kay found him within seconds.

"Are you all right?" she cried, running to him.

"All except my feet. I think they're frozen."

"Don't worry. Before you know it we'll have you in a warm place."

Then she remembered that the horse and sleigh were gone. She went back to look for the farmer, only to discover that he, too, had disappeared. Kay was on the verge of tears when she spotted the farmer coming toward her, leading the horse.

"Old Maud didn't go too far before she managed

to wedge the sleigh between two maple trees," he explained.

They lifted Bill into the sleigh, wrapped him in blankets and rushed him back to the farmhouse. The cold didn't seem to have done him any harm that the warmth of the farmhouse couldn't remedy. Soon his circulation was normal again. Kay was relieved to discover that his feet were not frozen, and that he would not likely suffer any permanent ill effects from his experience.

Now that Cousin Bill was out of danger, Kay could turn her attention to the three men who had left them in the burning cabin.

Her first move was to call the police station. Having made one futile trip that night the police were in no mood to answer a second call but Kay managed to persuade them that this time they would surely be able to make the arrest.

"If you'll meet me at Ike Stone's cabin near the railroad tracks, I think I can deliver the men into your hands," she promised. Kay was sure that the three would return to Stone and Blick's original hide-out.

Although Bill was in no condition to accompany her to the cabin, he insisted upon doing so and the farmer insisted on driving them. They stopped a short distance from the railroad tracks and there waited for the police.

"We've searched this cabin three times already," one of the policemen complained. "This is probably another false alarm."

The group cautiously approached the cabin. It seemed to be deserted. One of the officers pounded on the door, calling loudly:

"Open up, or we'll shoot!"

There was no response. They fired a warning shot

and pushed open the door. The cabin was empty!

"Just as I expected!" the captain of the squad said in disgust.

"Wait!" Kay commanded.

She moved swiftly to the trap-door and raised it. There was a sudden commotion below.

"I think we've got them," she said in satisfaction.

One of the officers descended into the basement and quickly discovered Bealing, Stone and Blick cowering behind a packing case. They were forced upstairs and handcuffed.

"You're responsible for this!" Bealing snapped, glowering at Kay.

"Oh, no," she returned calmly. "It was that six-fingered glove that gave you away."

"That extra finger!" he muttered angrily. "I knew it would some day prove to be my undoing. How I hate it! All my life I have been miserable because of it."

Kay told the policemen they ought to check one remaining packing case which had been stored in the basement.

"You meddler!" Ike Stone hissed. "If it hadn't been for you we would be free. You're like a cat with nine lives. You get out of boxes and a blazing cabin——"

"Shut up!" Blick ordered harshly. "Anything you say will be used as evidence against us."

"This box seems to be filled with movie equipment," remarked one of the officers.

"It belongs to the Eagle Film Company," Kay said, "and was stolen from a railroad car. They stole a lot of other equipment as well but I suppose it's been sold by now."

Stone and Blick emphatically denied the accusation. Nevertheless, they were taken to the police station with Bealing and locked up. Bill and Kay then went

home to a well-earned rest. Before retiring they related
to an excited household most of the story, leaving the
details for later.

Miss Ball and Clarence Minton arrived by airplane
from New York to help sew up the case. The actress
readily identified Bealing as the kidnaper and helped to
establish the fact that he was the same driver who had
hit Betty.

During the trial, it was brought out that some
months before Bealing had been turned down for a part
in one of Miss Ball's pictures. Brooding over this he had
pinned part of the blame on Clarence Minton.

That led him to plot revenge on both the manager
and the actress. Minton's near plane crash was the
handiwork of someone Bealing had paid to tamper with
the plane.

Kay was compelled to produce the letter she'd
received from Barbara Fountain. She was relieved to
learn, however, that the police had no intention of
tracking down Barbara's father but that he would be
allowed to make a fresh start in life.

Nathan Blick turned out to be a well-known thief.
Ike Stone did not have a previous criminal record but
had been Blick's willing accomplice. Lucy Cupp was
terribly upset when she was told that Stone had been
arrested. Though her involvement was innocent, she
assumed that she too would be arrested.

"When will the police come to arrest me?" Lucy
asked Kay tearfully.

"They won't. Not if you give up the ring."

"I don't want the diamond!" Lucy exclaimed
bitterly. "I hate the sight of it."

Soon after that, the ring was given over to the
police.

"I'm so glad everything is being taken care of so

quickly," Miss Ball declared. "With Bealing in jail I can rest easy. I'll be able to go back to work soon."

"I have just the play for you," Minton announced. "It will be a wonderful part for you. But I warn you, this may be your last professional appearance."

"My last?"

"I mean you are soon to become Mrs. Minton."

Miss Ball smiled warmly at Minton, but declared that she would never give up acting. Anticipating that response, Minton laughed good-naturedly.

The following morning the actress and her fiancée left for New York. In appreciation for all that Kay had done for them, Miss Ball pressed a small package into the girl's hand as they parted.

"It's a small gift," she told Kay, "to remind you of the exciting mystery you solved."

"It *was* exciting," Kay acknowledged, "but the best part of it all has been my friendship with you."

It wasn't until later that Kay opened the gift.

"A pair of kid gloves!" Kay exclaimed.

"They're beautiful!" Wendy said. "I'd wear them for dress. They're too good for school!"

The mention of school was a reminder that the Thanksgiving holidays were over; the following day they'd be back at Carmont High once more.

"Oh, well, Christmas will be coming soon," Kay said cheerfully. "Who knows? Perhaps we'll have another mystery on our hands by that time."

"Well, if you do, don't bring it to my house," Aunt Jane interposed, coming up behind the girls so quietly that they did not hear her. "I'm expecting you all back for Christmas, but I'm not inviting any black gloves!"

"Not even my new ones?" Kay laughed, giving her aunt a hug.

All too soon it was time for them to say good-bye.

Then Bill, Mrs. Tracey and the girls set off for Brantwood.

"Isn't this the night of the play?" Kay asked her friends.

"What play?" Betty asked.

"The one you bought tickets for. They were in the purse you lost the night you were hit by Bealing's car."

"I'd forgotten all about them! Let's go to the theater and see if anyone uses my tickets."

When the girls arrived at the theater they found the seats unoccupied. Presently, however, Kay's attention was drawn to three girls who were being escorted to their seats.

"Chris Eaton and two of her friends!" Betty exclaimed indignantly. "Why, the nerve of them! Chris must have known those tickets belonged to me because my name was in the purse."

"Let's play a joke on her," Kay proposed.

"I wish we could."

Kay hastily scribbled a note which she asked an usher to deliver to Chris. Chris read the note.

She whispered something to her friends and then they all left the theater, looking around nervously as they did so. Kay and her chums laughed so hard that they had trouble concentrating on the play which had just begun.

"What did you say in the note?" Betty finally asked.

"It was a very nice little note," Kay chuckled. "I merely wrote: 'I hope you enjoy the show.' But you see, I signed *your* name!"